His to
Protect

Elena Aitken

His to Protect: Bears of Grizzly Ridge, 1

Version 1.1

Ink Blot Communications
ISBN: 978-1-927968-43-7

Also by Elena

Grizzly Ridge
His to Protect
His to Seduce (Winter 2016)
His to Claim (Spring 2016)

The Springs
Summer of Change
Falling Into Forever
Winter's Burn
Midnight Springs
Second Glances
She's Making A List

Stone Summit Series
Summit of Desire
Summit of Seduction
Summit of Passion

For Ike,

My very own mountain man.

♥

CHAPTER ONE

Axel Jackson surveyed the land on the ridge and all he and his brothers had accomplished in the last nine months: The individual cabins tucked among the trees where he and his brothers lived. The barn that held a few trail riding horses. And of course the main lodge—the Den, they called it—that housed the guest rooms and main gathering spaces. They'd worked hard building a place they could call home. They'd had to.

More than that, they'd created a place they could build a life. If you called banishment from everything they'd known a life. But he did. As the eldest brother, and the alpha, there was no other choice.

He held the letter from his grandfather in his hand. The same letter he'd carried with him for almost a year. The patriarch of the clan, Gordon Jackson, was still old school when it came to communication. But it didn't matter how he chose to communicate; the message was just as old school.

Axel read the words he already knew by heart.

"Your failure to protect your clanmate, your sister, has resulted in your banishment from Jackson Valley. Until which time you and your brothers are able to return Kira, unharmed, to her proper clan, you will

no longer be welcome in the Valley or in the Clan."

He should rip it up and throw it into the wind. Instead, he folded it carefully along the timeworn crease lines. And just in time.

"I told you to throw that damn thing away," his brother Luke growled as he joined him on the ridge. His nakedness meant he'd recently been in his bear form. His preferred form. As shifters, they lived by a different code. Another reason the brothers had chosen the ridge to settle away from the others.

"Better yet," the youngest of the Jackson brothers, Kade, came to stand by Axel, "burn it."

Axel tucked it away into his pocket; Luke scoffed and shook his head. His scruffy, too-long long hair covered his eyes, but Axel could still see the disapproval there. "I don't know why you bother," he said. "The old man doesn't give a shit about us. He cast us out, the same way he cast out our parents. Giving him even a moment of our time is too much."

Everything his brother said was true. It wasn't the first time their grandfather had cast out a member. When their mother, Tonia, had fallen in love and subsequently chosen their father, Mark Chapman, who hailed from a rival clan, Gordon hadn't hesitated to banish her as well. Axel remembered very little about their parents, but he remembered more than the rest of them; he was five when they'd been sent back to the Jackson clan to live with their grandfather, and made to take the Jackson name again, forsaking the Chapman clan. He didn't know why or how it had come to pass, because no one would talk about it, but the fact remained: their grandfather was the only family they had.

"He's still family," he said to his brothers. "*Our* family."

"No," Kade said. "Family doesn't disown family because of a choice their sister makes." He winced and looked out over the ridge. Talking about Kira was hardest for Kade. As her twin brother, he felt the most that he'd let her down. Or perhaps that she'd been the one to let him down by choosing a mate in the first place. She'd known the consequences of her actions: alpha females in the Jackson clan didn't choose their own mates. Period. It was important to protect the lineage of the clan, and it was about more than producing cubs; it was more a business transaction between clan leaders than anything else. Which meant the granddaughter of the alpha male was promised. Not that it had mattered to Kira. She'd fallen in love. No matter what the cost had been to anyone else.

"Bear families do." Axel knew he was wasting his breath. It was the same argument they'd had for months. Ever since they'd tracked Kira the way they were told to. Only, instead of bringing her back to the clan the way their grandfather had commanded, they'd left her to live with her mate and his Kodiak clan. After hearing her story of fated mates, and how it felt as if their souls had chosen each other, the brothers agreed they had to leave her alone. All three of them had differing opinions about mating, but one thing none of them could deny was that forcing her to go with them and leave her mate would have been devastating to Kira. Never mind the war it likely would have sparked between the clans. None of the brothers were willing to do it. They'd decided then and there that together they'd accept whatever punishment their grandfather doled out.

No one had expected banishment.

Axel ran his hands through his thick hair. It had been months since he'd had it cut. A benefit to living on the ridge, as far as he was concerned. The bear in him preferred to live a bit wilder. Just not as wild as Luke, who still sat next to him naked, one leg bouncing restlessly. He was itching to take his leave so he could shift back into his bear and run through the woods. Luke was much harder to tame. The ridge lifestyle suited him most of all. He'd had the easiest time making the transition. Except when it came to potential mates. But that was part of the sacrifice. There were no females on the ridge. They were alone. Mating was less and less of an option.

A mate would calm the bear in all of them. And as the wildest of the three, Luke stood to benefit the most from mating. Not that he'd admit it. In fact, Luke would vehemently deny that he needed anything but the wilds of Montana and the freedom to do what he wanted. Kade sought his relief, however temporary, in the arms of whatever females he could find, driving down into town as often as he could. He'd be the hardest of all of them to convince that a mate could be a good thing. He'd seen firsthand the damage taking a mate could do, and as hardheaded as he was, there was no changing his mind.

As far as Axel was concerned, he wouldn't rule it out if the right female somehow appeared. Not that it was likely.

Whatever. He shook his head to focus on the task at hand. There was no point dwelling on what couldn't be changed. "Is everything ready?"

Kade turned back to face him. The quietest of the three, sullen and almost angry, he'd become even more withdrawn in the last nine months. His dark eyes always looked a little haunted, a little sad. It was the loss of Kira. Twin bears had a unique bond, one even Axel couldn't hope to understand. It would be better if he let himself grieve her loss. If he'd let himself feel anything. But Kade seemed to have inflicted his own brand of punishment upon himself. "I brought the last of the supplies up on my last run to town. Everything should be in place. All we need now are guests."

When they'd decided to stay on the ridge, the brothers had come up with the idea to create an eco-tourism lodge that focused on hiking in the summer and backcountry skiing in the winter. It would be the first of its kind in Montana: rugged enough to appeal to the adventurous spirit, but cushy enough to be an upscale destination. It was the perfect compromise for the brothers. They may not be able to go home to Jackson Valley to the lives they'd left behind, but it wouldn't stop them from creating new ones.

"It's taken care of." Axel smiled. "We have some registered guests coming later in the week, but you guys are going to love this…"

"What are we going to love?"

"Try to restrain your bear for a few days," he said to Luke. "Because I secured a travel journalist from LA who's going to write a feature on Grizzly Ridge for *Lifestyles Magazine*."

"No shit?" That impressed Luke the way Axel knew it would.

"It's true. And she's going to be here in the morning with a guest. So seriously, rein in your bear."

Luke grumbled and kicked the ground, but Axel knew he'd do as he was told. They may have chosen the ridge for its remoteness and ability to shift into their bear form whenever they needed to, but now that there would be humans around, everyone was going to have to be a lot more careful.

Harper Bentley pulled into her garage and closed it behind her before she got out of the car. The thought of staying inside with her vehicle running flashed through her brain for a second. But only a second. She wouldn't give that asshole husband of hers the satisfaction.

Ex-husband.

Well, maybe not yet. But soon. Very soon.

Harper slammed the door to the garage and entered the

relative peace of her home. Relative being the key word. Nothing about her house was peaceful. It was cold and glass and...decidedly not hers. It was Trent's. He'd designed and built it for appearances. Just like everything else in his life.

Until now.

With a sigh of disgust, Harper grabbed a bottle of wine from the rack, quickly popped the cork and poured herself a big glass before once more pulling the newspaper from her purse. It was already open to page four. The society pages. *Where everyone who was anyone made an appearance.* That's what Trent always said and look at him now. By the size of the photo, it was clear that Trent Bentley, co-owner of Bentley Images and Public Relations, was definitely someone. A very *gay* someone.

She tipped the glass back and swallowed half the contents easily in one gulp.

Trent's coming out was already a social sensation. Everyone was talking about it. Too bad they were also talking about her and how as the operating partner of Bentley Images, Harper Bentley clearly didn't have any kind of handle on image or public relations. It hadn't taken long for the media to spin everything in favor of Trent, the sophisticated and trendy gay man, braving society and coming out with his boyfriend, Blake Johnson. Which meant that same media had also done a superior job portraying Bentley as the dumpy, unaware, and completely clueless public relations representative who obviously couldn't handle any of her high-profile clients if she couldn't even handle herself. It had taken less than an hour after Trent's *big reveal* to go public for her phone to ring with five of her biggest clients dropping her.

"No doubt to go to the dark side," she muttered and finished off the rest of her wine. And it hadn't taken long for the reporters to get a hold of that information, too.

Professionally, she was effectively dead. Never mind personally, not that Trent's sexual orientation had been much of a surprise. However, his betrayal had been.

Harper grabbed the bottle to pour herself another glass. "Oh, screw it." Forgoing the glass, she tipped the bottle up to her mouth.

"Nicely done."

The voice startled her and she choked on the wine. When she recovered from the ensuing coughing fit, she turned and glared at her best friend, Nina. "That wasn't nice."

"I'm the least of your problems," she said. "Besides, you gave me a key for a reason. I wasn't about to let you drink yourself into oblivion by yourself."

Harper pushed the bottle away. Nina was right. She was infuriating, but she was right. There was a reason they'd been best friends for years. "How did you know?"

"About the drinking? Or Trent?"

"Both." She thought better of her hasty decision and reached for the bottle again, but Nina held it out of reach.

"You know I've known about Trent for years." Harper nodded and didn't look up. They'd both known. But not right away. At first, it just seemed as though he just hadn't wanted to have sex. He was too tired, or not feeling good, or had a bad back. But then it was other things, too. On the rare occasions they actually did have sex, it was terrible. More than terrible. Harper may not have had a lot of experience with men, but she knew enough to know it was supposed to be better than that. They'd only been married two years when Trent finally admitted he'd married her as a cover. She'd been hurt, certainly. She should have left him then and she knew it. But something kept her, and as loathe as she was to admit it, that something was low self-esteem. She'd always been so strong in every other way, but when it came to feeling attractive or desirable, well, that was different. If she left Trent in search of something *more,* there wasn't any guarantee she'd find it. At least if she stayed, she'd have *something.* It was weak and she knew it. Over the years, she hated herself a little bit more for not allowing herself to go after what she deserved. But it became a vicious cycle she just couldn't seem to get out of.

Not that it was all bad. Their business was finally taking off. They were successful, getting more clients all the time. They worked well together. They were partners, friends, and their relationship was good.

Except for that one small detail.

She should have known once he'd met Blake it would only be a matter of time. He'd had boyfriends over the ten years they'd been married. Most of them discreet, but Blake had been different. *Dammit.* She should have been strong enough to leave him years ago. On her own terms. She should have been— "Give me the wine."

Nina shook her head. "No deal. I know this sucks and you're probably sitting there thinking of all the things you should have done differently." Harper shrugged. "But getting drunk isn't going to help."

"It's not going to hurt." She glared at her best friend. "But you're right. It's not the solution." The actual solution came to her in a flash and she pushed up from the chair to head for the fridge. "It's not like I have an image to worry about anymore. I'm going to eat whatever I want. Starting with this." She pulled out half a cheesecake that Trent had brought home a few nights before. Likely to torture her. Knowing she couldn't eat it on her diet. Her perpetual diet. It didn't seem to matter what she did—she had curves. Too many curves for Los Angeles, that was for sure.

Screw it. Her career was already circling the drain. Harper grabbed a fork and dug in, savoring the first bite.

"Well, at least share with me." Nina took the fork from her hand and took her own bite before she handed it back. "Because I have just the medicine you need."

Harper raised her eyebrows. "I don't know if drugs are really the answer right now, Nina."

"Stop it." Nina smacked her and laughed. "I'm totally serious."

"And what is the medicine you offer exactly? Because I need something."

"I have an assignment to do, and the offer was for two people. You're going to be my plus one." Nina was a travel writer and always jetting off to fabulous places where she was wined and dined. And got paid for it. Harper could definitely go for some wining and dining. Especially if it was far away from Los Angeles. Nina grabbed the fork again, but instead of taking another bite, she tossed it in the sink. "Come on. You have to pack. We're leaving first thing in the morning."

"What?" Harper let herself be dragged into the bedroom. She had neither the strength nor the desire to stop it. Especially if it meant a lavish holiday. "Where are we going?"

Nina turned and grinned. "Montana, baby."

Something was in the air.

Axel hadn't been able to sleep and it wasn't just the anticipation of their first guests. It was something else. Something in his blood that had kept him up. His bear was restless. He had too much to do, and the helicopter was due to land in less than an hour with the journalist. He couldn't afford to run off into the woods to satiate the animal inside him. There wasn't time.

Still…he couldn't afford not to.

Naked, Axel stepped outside into the dewy summer morning. Even on what would be a hot day, the mornings in the mountains were still cool. *Perfect.* He left behind the steps of his cabin and shifted seamlessly into his bear as he took off for the woods in long, lumbering strides.

He wouldn't be gone long. Just long enough to calm his bear.

As soon as he hit the trees, he increased his pace, pushing himself farther, harder, faster. His muscles strained with the effort and the exertion was just what he needed to quiet his brain and soothe his spirit.

A scent on the air caught his attention. Luke was somewhere in the distance but he wasn't surprised. Luke spent as much time as possible in his bear form and with the impending arrival of guests on the ridge, the opportunity to shift wouldn't be as forthcoming. Not that Axel was worried about it. They'd all lived among humans in the valley. It had never been a problem. Well, not really.

Where Luke was concerned, there was always a problem or two. All he needed to do was minimize them, at least while guests were around.

Axel growled and snuffed the air as he continued to lumber through the woods. He slowed his pace and pulled up as he arrived at the edge of the forest where the sky opened up to the valley below. The view never failed to calm him. Whenever he was worked up about something, he somehow always found his way to the edge of the mountain to find perspective. He sat heavy on his haunches and inhaled the fresh morning air. In his bear, all his senses were heightened, a little more alive. It generally made it easier to relax, but the stillness he'd hoped for didn't come right away. He took another breath. An eagle shrieked as it soared through the valley.

Still, his bear couldn't be calmed. Not the way he needed it to be.

And he knew why.

At thirty and the oldest of the brothers, Axel was due to take a mate first. In fact, he should have found one years ago. It was the only way for shifters to keep their animal side satiated. But even before banishment, he hadn't found a female who was right for him. Of course, his grandfather, the alpha of the clan, had tried to impose upon him a deadline to find his own mate, or he'd be mated to a female from a neighboring clan. The bloodline had to be preserved. Not that it mattered. Since the banishment, it hadn't been an issue.

Except it was.

Not that either of them seemed to think it was a problem. None of them except Axel. No matter. They were all going to have to find a way to distract themselves for the time being. At least until a solution presented itself.

Just then, Axel's ears tuned in to the sound of a helicopter. *Perfect. Their first guests would be just the distraction he needed.*

It started as a grumble deep inside, but quickly built in strength and intensity until Axel opened his impressive jaws and let out the roar inside until it echoed against the valley walls as the helicopter dipped and flew directly overhead.

"Did you see that?"

Harper had been staring out the window from the moment they'd taken off. She'd never been in a helicopter before and the view was incredible. She whacked Nina on the arm in an effort to get her attention, but she was still intently focused on her phone and frantically tapped a message on the tiny keyboard.

"Nina." Harper shook her sleeve. "Seriously. There are bears out there. Look!"

She pointed again to the ridge and the giant grizzly she'd seen a moment earlier up on his hind legs. Obviously, she couldn't hear anything, but Harper knew the grizzly was roaring. It sent a shiver through her entire body and straight to her core.

Wow, it had been awhile since she'd been laid. The fact that she could find a wild animal—a bear—even slightly arousing was definitely a sign that she needed to scratch an itch. In a very bad way. And that's just what she'd do…as soon as she was done on the mountain with Nina.

Who was *still* on her phone!

"Nina! Seriously. Look at that bear." She pointed out the window where the bear in question had turned and ran back through the woods. As the helicopter flew overhead, the animal almost seemed to keep pace. Harper knew she was having a once-in-a-lifetime experience. To be able to see a grizzly so close up was amazing. And oddly exhilarating. "He's gorgeous!"

"Gorgeous?" That got her friend's attention. "Only you would talk about an animal that way. You're such a horn dog. You seriously need to have sex. With a man," she added and Harper rolled her eyes. Nina leaned across Harper and looked out the window. "You're totally right though. That is a magnificent specimen."

Harper laughed. "Now who's a horn dog?"

"I'm just saying." She shrugged. "Maybe we'll get to see one in person. It is called Grizzly Ridge, after all."

"I hope we don't," Harper said even though she did secretly hope they'd see a bear up close. "They're dangerous and that's not exactly the type of holiday I was hoping to have." In fact, she hadn't been hoping to have the kind of holiday where she was stranded at the top of a mountain in a lodge in the middle of nowhere Montana, either. But beggars couldn't be choosers. And even if it wasn't one of Nina's posh spa assignments, she'd take it. Anything to get away from her life for a bit.

Harper turned to look back at the bear, but she couldn't spot him again. He must have been swallowed up in the forest as the helicopter moved toward the landing pad. It was a good thing anyway. Bears were dangerous. It was probably for the best if he kept his distance.

CHAPTER TWO

"Where've you been?" Kade sniffed the air in Axel's direction as he jogged down to the main lodge to join his brothers.

"I'm not late."

"That's not what I asked."

Axel shrugged off the question. They had more important things to do this morning than discuss the practicality of shifting when they were expecting their first guests. But there'd been no help for it. "Let's go," he said instead. "They're going to land any second."

They jumped into the Jeep with Luke already behind the wheel. They'd decided it was probably best for all of them to be there to meet the reporters. Luke and Kade would walk back to the lodge while Axel got their guests settled.

It was only a short drive and sure enough, when they pulled up, the helicopter had just touched down. The blades sputtered their final spin as it powered down.

"Here goes nothing." Luke turned off the ignition and opened the door.

"No." Axel stopped him. "Here goes everything. This is going to work. Grizzly Ridge is going to become the premier eco-tourism destination in Montana. Even more

14

so than that damned dude ranch, or whatever it is, down the valley." He shook off the small matter of their competition. "And we're going to be happy." He added the last bit more for himself than his brothers. Keeping themselves busy with the running of the Ridge would be the perfect distraction to keep their bears settled.

Hopefully.

All three Jackson brothers, doing their best to look presentable, strode toward the helicopter. The pilot opened the back door and a thin blonde woman with a messenger bag slung over her shoulder hopped out.

"Hi," the woman said. "I'm Nina." She stuck out her hand and Axel took it first. "Nina Renton. I'm happy to be here to check out your new business. Thanks for the invitation."

She was spunky and full of energy. *Perfect*. With any luck, she'd be excited about everything Grizzly Ridge had to offer and write a glowing article about them.

"It's nice to meet you. I'm Axel Jackson." He flashed her a grin. "This is my brother Luke—he's our hiking and backcountry specialist—and our youngest brother, Kade. He handles most of the guest comforts. Anything you need, please don't hesitate to—"

He couldn't finish his thought because, just over Nina's shoulder, another woman appeared. And not just any woman, but one with a scent like no other. A combination of spice with a touch of sweet apple that flooded his senses. Every muscle in Axel's body tensed, the blood in his veins ran hotter, and his bear threatened to roar a claim on the curvy blonde goddess who'd just appeared before him.

His mate.

15

Wow. Harper wasn't sure what to expect at Grizzly Ridge, but it sure as hell hadn't been three freakin' hot men waiting for them when they got out of the helicopter. Clearly they built them big, strong, and sexy as fuck in the mountains. Maybe the Montana trip would be just as good as a posh spa trip after all.

"This is my friend, Harper Bentley," Nina introduced her. "She needed a holiday so she decided to come with me to check things out." She waved her hand at the trio of men. "Luke, Kade, and Axel."

The first two men shook her hand, but when she turned to face the third, a shiver went through her and she instinctively took a step back. His imposing body stood over her, a solid mass of muscle; two dark eyes bored into her. His mouth was pressed into a firm line and the muscles in his jaw twitched with the obvious tension he held. *Was it her? Had she not been expected?* Well, she was here now. Like it or not, she wasn't going anywhere. So he'd just have to make the best of it. As would she. Harper jutted out her hand. "Axel, was it? Nice to meet you."

His gaze ran over her as if he was drinking in every bit of her. But instead of it making her feel uneasy, his appraisal warmed her. Harper straightened her shoulders, which had the effect of thrusting her ample breasts out. She could have sworn she heard a low growl from somewhere, but it was forgotten the instant Axel took her hand and squeezed. It was ridiculous, but an electric heat shot through her at his touch, directly down to the cleft between her legs.

He held on a beat too long, but as far as Harper was concerned he could have held her hand all day if it meant sparking that type of response in her.

One of the other brothers, whose name she couldn't recall at the moment, cleared his throat and physically pulled Axel back. "We should get you ladies settled into the Den."

"The Den? That sounds cozy." Nina laughed. Harper noticed absently that she had her notebook out and was already taking notes.

"It's really the main lodge," the man—Luke, Harper remembered—said. "We like to call it the Den as part of the whole Grizzly experience." He winked at Nina and glanced at Harper with a question on his face.

She was still slightly stunned at the effect Axel had on her, but she tripped her way along the dirt path after them as Luke led them to a truck. She slid inside when he held the door open for them and Nina scrambled in after her. The second the door was closed, her friend spun and stared at her.

"What was that all about?"

"What are you talking about?"

"Don't even try it," Nina said. "You know damn well what I'm talking about. What was that between you and Axel? He was staring at you as if he could just eat you up. Damn, girl."

Harper shook her head. Not her. Men didn't look at her like that. They looked at Nina like that, certainly. But not her. She always had just a few extra pounds on her, and enough strong will to intimidate most men. "I probably reminded him of someone is all."

"Well, it must have been someone important because it seems to be causing a bit of a fuss." Nina pointed out the Jeep window and Harper turned just in time to see Kade grab Axel's arm only moments before Axel tried to swing a punch in Luke's direction. "They're fighting about you."

That made Harper laugh. She tried to stifle her snort. "Men don't fight over or about me. It must be some brother thing."

"Whatever it is, they sure are a bit on the wild side up here in the mountains," Nina said. "And hot. Oh, so deliciously hot. And that one is clearly into you. Sounds just about right for a fling, if you ask me."

Harper didn't have time to counter her friend's comment because just then the driver's side door opened and Kade hopped in behind the wheel. "I hope you ladies don't mind me driving you up to the Den and getting you settled in. Axel was hoping to be the one to do that, but it turns out he has a bit of business to take care of."

"No problem," Nina purred and Harper tried not to roll her eyes.

There was definitely a twinge of regret or disappointment or something in her gut at the thought that it wasn't Axel with them, but no doubt she'd see him again. She twisted in her seat to look out the back window. Just in time to see Axel storm off toward the tree line.

What kind of business could he possibly have in the forest?

She certainly didn't have much experience with mountain men—none, really. But from what she could see, they were definitely more interesting than any men she'd come across lately. And Nina was right: oh so deliciously hot.

"Axel!"

He ignored the call of his brother and kept moving into the cover of the trees. He couldn't shift but dammit, he wanted to. No, he *needed* to.

That female. Her scent. Her touch. Her *everything*. He hadn't been prepared for that. Hell, nothing could have prepared him for that. She was his mate. But she was a human. *Wasn't she? Maybe not…there was something about her*

18

scent... No. It wasn't possible.

Axel roared and spun as his brother's hand clamped down on his shoulder.

"Easy, big guy," Luke said, but he wasn't joking. The look in his younger brother's eyes was all business. "You need to settle down."

With another roar, he wound up and punched the trunk of a nearby pine. The tree rocked and split from the force; Axel's knuckles burned with the crush of bone. No matter—it would be healed in minutes.

"Feel better?" Luke leaned up against a nearby tree, his arms crossed.

Axel nodded begrudgingly. "A little." It was far from ideal, but if he couldn't shift—and he couldn't, not with humans so close by—getting physical was the next best option.

"Good," Luke said. "Now, do you want to talk about what just happened back there?"

Axel shook his head and growled. *Talk about it?*
Hell no.

That was the last thing he wanted to do. He couldn't talk about something that he didn't understand. And he didn't understand what had just happened. Not even a little bit. He'd never reacted to a female that way.

Never.

Especially a human female.

"Fine by me," Luke said. "But you're going to need to pull your shit together and quickly because you can't go acting all...animal around our guests." He waited a beat; Axel took a breath and paced back to where his brother stood. "You good?"

Axel nodded.

"Good. Let's go. I don't want to leave Kade in charge of entertaining those two for too long. Who knows what will happen."

It was a good point. Kade had a bit of a reputation of being a…well, to call a spade a spade, when he wasn't being all brooding and grouchy, Kade was a man whore. And unashamed about it, too. At least he had been before Kira took off. Luke and Axel were both fully aware that Kade made regular visits down the mountain to the local pub where he *entertained* women; he just didn't talk about it anymore. Things had changed with Kade. He was far more secretive and withdrawn now. His sexual conquests were more of a penance than a release and Axel knew exactly why that was. His little brother hadn't let his bear out since Kira left. It had been almost a year. Way too long for a bear shifter to go without recognizing his true self. It would be torture for Kade. A torture he seemed to think he deserved.

Either way, Axel didn't want his sexually charged brother anywhere near his female. "Let's go," he grunted and led the way back through the trees. It only took him a minute to realize he'd already referred to the curvy blonde as *his* female.

CHAPTER THREE

The main lodge, or Den as it was called, was both cozy and luxurious in a rustic, mountain kind of way. The main living area had vaulted timber beam ceilings and a huge rock fireplace at one end. In the back of the building was a well-stocked gourmet kitchen, where the ladies were told to help themselves to anything at any time, and off to the side was a dining room where everyone would eat, family-style. "Your rooms are just up the stairs here." Kade led them back through the main room to a spiral staircase that was constructed from the same wood beams as the rest of the Den. At the top of the stairs were six doors, presumably all leading to bedrooms.

"Do you all stay up here, too?" Harper hoped the question sounded a lot more casual than it did in her head but she was curious. Mostly about the dark-haired, ridiculously handsome brother who'd held her hand in hers before he'd disappeared. He'd sparked an electricity in her like she hadn't felt in years. No, scratch that. She hadn't felt that type of connection from a man *ever*. It couldn't possibly hurt to get a few details about him.

"No." Kade shook his head. "We all have our own cabins out back. It's better to have a little bit of privacy sometimes."

Harper shook her head at the obvious way the man was eyeing up Nina. Not that her friend noticed anything. Nina certainly liked to have fun, but when she was on assignment, nothing would distract her. Especially if she thought it might cloud her opinion of what she was working on.

"I like it." Nina scratched something down in her notebook. "Which one is my room?"

All business. Harper dutifully followed them up the stairs, only half listening while Nina rattled off a series of questions. Before going into the room Kade pointed out as hers, she paused and took another look around, hoping Axel had appeared. Still nothing. Not that it mattered, she told herself. It didn't.

A spark was just that. A spark. It wasn't anything more than that. If it was even that. It was entirely likely it had just been so long since she'd been touched by a man that her body didn't know how to react.

Yes. That was probably it.

With a sigh, she left Nina, who was still peppering Kade with questions about the amenities in her room, and retreated to her own space. She was pleasantly surprised with the room. It wasn't overly large, but it had the same rustic charm the rest of the Den had. She sat and bounced on the bed. *Not bad. Comfy and it would be just the right size for two...* She let the thought drift away.

How did she manage to go from a handshake to a romp in the bed? Harper flopped back on the bed and groaned just as the door opened.

"What's wrong?"

She didn't bother to sit up and look at Nina, not that it mattered because a moment later, her best friend laid down next to her. Harper turned and propped her head up on her elbow. "Nothing." She sighed. "Okay, everything."

Nina laughed. "No kidding. But this trip will help. I promise. What do you think so far?"

"Gorgeous." Harper didn't clarify about who or what exactly she thought was gorgeous, but judging by the way Nina wiggled her eyebrows, she'd figured it out.

"Right? Maybe that's just the brand of gorgeous you need to distract yourself right now?"

Harper sat up and stared at her friend. "I can't do that!"

"Why not? It's not like you're working. Cut loose and have some fun."

"I've never done anything like that," Harper protested. She wasn't the type to have a random fling with someone. At least she never had been the type. Of course, she'd been married to a gay man for the last ten years.

"Harper. Seriously." Nina sat up and stared at her. "The only reason you haven't done anything like that before is because you have some warped sense of commitment. If you ask me, you should have let loose years ago. You are way overdue for some fun. And an orgasm."

Harper groaned. Nina was right. She was way overdue for an orgasm, that was for sure. "Okay," she said before she realized the word had come out of her mouth. "Why not? And you're right. I need to have a little fun."

Nina clapped her hands and bounced on the bed. "Perfect, because tonight, after the scheduled activities, apparently there's a group dinner and drinks downstairs. Everyone should be there." She wiggled her eyebrows again.

"Everyone? As in..."

"All the brothers. I saw the way you looked at Axel and I don't think anyone missed the way he was looking at you. I swear I almost heard him growl."

Harper laughed and went to look at herself in the

mirror. In her skinny jeans and cotton t-shirt that hugged all her curves in just the right places, she did look good. She flipped her hair back over her shoulder, turned and offered a hand to Nina. "Well, let's get on with it then. The sooner this day is over, the sooner it will be dinner time."

For the majority of the day, Axel had managed to avoid Harper. Not that he wanted to. Hell, what he wanted was exactly the opposite. His animal wanted to hunt her down and claim her. Hard and fast. Which was exactly why he needed to keep his distance. He couldn't risk the future of Grizzly Ridge just because he had some sort of urge.

Some sort of urge. He snorted as he stepped into the hot shower. That was an understatement.

It was more than an urge. A lot more. From the moment he laid eyes on Harper and scented her on the air, his bear had been wide awake and ready to roar. It wasn't an urge. It was a primal need to have the woman.

"Dammit." Axel turned and cranked the tap to the right. A hot shower wasn't going to help a dammed thing. The icy water hit him with a sting, but it had little effect on calming his desire.

After rushing through his shower, Axel tried to figure out how to get out of joining the group for dinner. It would be pure torture to sit across from Harper, with those round, full breasts straining against her t-shirt, just waiting for him to reach over and tear the thin cotton from her— *no*. He had to stop letting those thoughts in. They'd been driving him crazy all day and it was beyond ridiculous considering he didn't know a single thing about her. Except her name.

And her scent.

24

That was enough.

A knock on his cabin door distracted him from his thoughts, which was a damn good thing considering they were only taking a turn for the dirtier.

"Who's there?"

The door opened and Luke walked in. "I see you're still in a mood."

Axel glared at him but didn't deny it as he grabbed a shirt from his drawer and pulled it over his head. "What do you want?"

"Time for dinner. You need to be there."

"Not going."

"To hell you're not." Luke leaned his bulk against the doorframe and crossed his arms. "You're supposed to be the face of Grizzly Ridge and so far you've spent the entire day hiding in the woods like a little—" He broke off when Axel growled at him. "Whatever," Luke said. "Get your ass in gear. You're coming."

"Try not to forget who's in charge here." Axel rarely pulled rank. It wasn't usually an issue. Of course, he'd never had the scent of his potential mate driving him crazy before. "I make the decisions around here."

"Right." Luke clenched his jaw and pushed up from the doorjamb. "Well, *boss*. I'm sure you'll feel good about your decision to skip dinner knowing that for the last hour, since their hike, our guests have been in the Den. The reporter started working on her piece, but her friend, Harper"—Luke paused and made eye contact with his brother—"she's been in the kitchen, drinking wine and helping Kade cook."

At the mention of Harper spending time with Kade, especially if alcohol was involved, Axel's bear reared up. Jealousy and protectiveness overwhelmed him. He shoved his feet into his boots and without another word, pushed past Luke on the way out of the cabin.

"That's what I thought," he heard Luke mutter, but he didn't bother turning around. He had bigger problems: if Kade laid one hand on his female, he'd kill him. Brother or not.

CHAPTER FOUR

Harper watched as Kade poured her another glass of wine. She shouldn't be drinking so much, so fast, but she couldn't help it. The wine tasted fabulous. Besides, she was on vacation. And Nina was right: she deserved to have a little fun. Maybe even a lot of fun.

Too bad she hadn't seen Axel all day. Not since that first meeting. Kade said something about how his oldest brother was in charge of running things at Grizzly Ridge, which made it seem even stranger that he'd totally vanished, but she wasn't going to dwell on it. She'd had a good time on the hike Luke led them on. The mountains really were beautiful and so peaceful. She'd been completely energized by the time outdoors and when Nina excused herself to rest and write, Harper had been too keyed up to do the same.

Thankfully, Kade had been good company. She was perched on a stool at the counter of the gourmet kitchen, watching him prepare what started to smell as if it would be a mouthwatering dinner.

She lifted the glass to her lips and took another deep sip. "I probably shouldn't be drinking so much before I've had something to eat." She giggled. "How many glasses is

27

that, now?"

"Nobody's counting." Kade winked at her and flashed a toothy grin. "You're on holidays." He was handsome. Very handsome. He had the same rugged good looks as his brothers. They all looked so similar, yet so incredibly different at the same time. Luke was fair, almost like a California surfer, while Kade's hair was darker, more of a chestnut with gold flecks. He was a bit shorter than the others, although all three of them loomed over Harper's five seven. She'd never considered herself to be short, but compared to the Jackson brothers, she felt positively petite. And then there was Axel. Dark and dangerous. At least that had been her immediate impression when he'd touched her. His eyes were such a deep brown they almost looked black when they'd bored into her, locking her gaze. A chill went through her just thinking of Axel and the sizzle she'd felt from him.

"Are you cold? I can light a fire in the main room." Kade grabbed a towel and wiped his hands. "Let me just—"

"No," she interrupted him. She didn't want to sit in the living room by herself. Not when she was enjoying the company so much. She certainly didn't have the same attraction to Kade as she did his older brother, but the more time that went by without seeing Axel, the more she couldn't help but think she'd imagined their connection. Besides, it's not as though she had a lifetime to spend at Grizzly Ridge. She was only going to be there for a few days and dammit if she didn't have an itch to scratch. Axel definitely would be her first choice, but she was tired of men who didn't want her.

Maybe it was the alcohol, or maybe she was just sick and tired of not going after what she wanted. Or thought she wanted. Whatever it was, before she could overthink it, Harper reached out and grabbed Kade's arm. "I'm fine," she said. "I'd rather stay right here."

Kade's eyes sparked. He was a smart man and clearly caught on quickly. His lip quirked up in a grin. "Sounds good to me," he said. "Sounds very—"

"Kade!"

The swinging door to the kitchen crashed open. Harper jumped off her stool and spilled her wine on the floor. Axel's bulk filled the doorway and even from across the room, Harper could see his eyes darken. Fear flashed through her and instinctively she took a step back just as Kade stood tall and crossed his arms across his chest. "Axel," he said calmly.

With two long strides, Axel crossed the room and stood toe-to-toe with his brother. From up close, the size difference between the two was obvious. Axel loomed over him, and his obvious anger made him seem even larger. Or more ferocious. Either way, Harper took another step back. "Keep your paws off my"—he glanced quickly in her direction—"*our* guest," he spoke through clenched teeth.

"Settle down, big guy." Kade held his hands up in front of him. It was obvious he was trying, but failing, in an effort not to smile. "I was just keeping Harper company and sharing some wine. Don't get all—"

"It looked like a lot more than that."

Was that jealousy in his voice? A thrill went through her. She'd never had anyone be jealous over her before. Even if it was unwarranted. Or was it? Hadn't she just been considering Kade as an alternative to his brother for a fling? Although now that she saw Axel again, she couldn't imagine what she'd been thinking. Her whole body reacted to his presence, from the tips of her fingers that itched to reach out and touch him, all the way to the damp spot between her legs. Oh yes, there was no doubt her body had a reaction to this man. A strong one.

"It was nothing." Harper stepped forward. Axel turned to her and their eyes locked. Her stomach flipped and she had to swallow hard. "I was just telling Kade I was a bit chilly and he suggested a fire in the great room. Maybe you'd like to light it for me?" She took another step until she stood right in front of him, so close they almost touched, and she could feel the heat radiate off him. *Forget the fire. All she needed was Axel.* Preferably naked and in her bed.

One thing at a time.

Harper forced what she hoped was an innocent smile. "If you wouldn't mind?" She reached out and let her fingers trail lightly across his bare forearm.

If I wouldn't mind? Axel's brain raced; his heart beat even harder. *If I wouldn't mind indeed,* he thought. *I wouldn't mind throwing you over my shoulder and marching your sweet ass right out of here is what I wouldn't mind.*

He swallowed and caught her hand in his. "I wouldn't mind at all."

And just like that, the jealous rage he'd felt when he'd burst into the kitchen and seen Kade touching his female was gone. Her touch had calmed him while at the same time energizing him. It was unlike anything he'd ever felt before. He didn't move right away, and it wasn't until Kade cleared his throat loudly and shoved a bottle of wine and two glasses at them that Axel released Harper's hand and stepped back.

"Enjoy," his brother said with an obvious laugh in his voice. "Dinner will be ready soon."

He led the way out into the great room and poured

them each a glass before he turned his attention to the fireplace. He spent a little longer than absolutely necessary building the fire up but he needed the time to gather his thoughts together. Never before had he felt such a pull toward a female. And he knew she felt something too. He could smell her arousal on the air. It was a heady, sweet scent that filled his senses and made it even harder to focus on the task at hand.

He was an expert fire starter, but he fumbled through the process. Finally, when the fire was roaring, he backed away and turned to see her lounging with her legs curled up underneath her on the large leather sofa. She wore an oversized sweater that hid too much of her beautiful body from his eyes, but he let his eyes linger on the swell of her ass and the length of her legs that were covered in form-fitting denim. He swallowed a growl at the idea of running his hands along those curves and tearing the clothing from her body until he could see every inch of her.

"That's hot."

Axel started. *Had she read his thoughts?*

"The fire," she clarified with a laugh. "It's hot. Thank you. I'm not chilly anymore." She sat up and pulled her sweater over her head to reveal the very same skintight t-shirt that had formed an integral part of his daydream. His bear roared within him. He wanted—no, he needed—to claim this woman.

Judging from the way she looked at him, and the seductive way she ran her tongue along her lower lip, she knew exactly what effect she had on him. *Well, maybe not exactly the effect*, he thought as he forced his bear to stay calm, *but if she wasn't careful, she was going to find out.*

"I'm glad I could help." He crossed the room, and despite the fact that he knew exactly how dangerous it was to be in close proximity, he took his glass of wine and sat next to her on the couch. "Are you enjoying your time at the Ridge so far?"

She nodded but then shook her head.

"You're not?"

"No," she said quickly. "I am. But I couldn't help but wonder where you were today?" She bit her lip and Axel had to look away to keep himself from biting it, too.

"I was working." He took a healthy swallow of wine. "But I'm here now." And he couldn't imagine being anywhere else. He'd been a fool to stay away from her all day. Yes, keeping his hands off her was going to prove to be challenging, but just being in her presence tamed his bear in a way that it'd never been before. It would be worth the effort of behaving. "Is there anything I can do for you to make your stay even more enjoyable?"

You could throw me down on this couch, slide those big hands up my body and kiss me like I was the last woman on earth. That might make my stay a little more enjoyable.

Harper swallowed hard and forced herself not to look away. She was playing way outside her comfort zone. Maybe it was the wine giving her just enough courage, or the wildness of the mountains, or the fact that she really had nothing to lose, but she'd never been very good at flirting with men—or doing anything with men, really. Staying married to Trent had done a number on her self-esteem and in the not so distant past, she would never have considered such open flirting with a man. But she'd never had a man like Axel in front of her before. He brought out something totally different in her. Something she wanted to explore further.

"You look like you want to say something," he said after

a moment. His dark eyes sparkled with humor. He knew damn well what she wanted to say.

She took another gulp of wine, set the glass down and turned to face him. *Here goes nothing.* "I think it would make my stay a lot more comfortable if you kissed me."

The second the words were out of her mouth, Harper could hardly believe she'd said them. But it was almost as if speaking her desire gave her more power because, to her surprise, she wasn't even remotely worried about his response. Especially because the moment she spoke, his eyes darkened with desire. Before she could spare another thought for how he might react, he reached out, wrapped his hand around her arm and pulled her toward him until their faces were only inches apart. "I think I might be able to help you out with that." His voice was low and deep and caused a rush of heat through her body. And then his lips were on hers, hungry and hot. A sound, something between a sigh and a moan, escaped her lips. It only seemed to encourage him, and the kiss deepened.

This could get out of hand very quickly.

Perfect.

She reached up with the desperate need to run her hands through his hair and tug him closer, but before she could, he jerked away. Seconds later, Nina's voice rang out in the hallway above them.

"Harper! Where are you? You've got to see this."

She stared at Axel. *Had he heard Nina coming? How was it even possible?* She wanted to ask him, but before she could get the words out, he hopped up off the couch.

"I'm sorry," he said.

"Sorry?"

He bent down, so only she could hear him. "I shouldn't have done that."

"Shouldn't have—"

"There you are."

Harper turned away from Axel to see Nina running down the stairs. She turned back, but Axel was at the fire, his strong, broad back to her as he fed more logs in. *Shouldn't have done what?* She wanted to scream. He should have done exactly that. And more. Her body burned with the heat he'd ignited in her. She wanted more. Needed more.

"Harper?"

Right. Nina. She turned back to her friend, who looked at her as if she'd lost her mind. "What?"

"You have to see this." Nina thrust an iPad into her hands.

She scanned the website in front of her. "What am I looking at?"

"This." Nina jabbed a finger at the screen. "Bentley Images and Public Relations is under investigation for fraud and embezzlement. Look."

The hair on the back of her neck pricked up and the room suddenly got very cold.

"What?" She scanned the article. And then again. With every word she read, it got harder to breathe. "I don't…what…where is this from?"

"It's the *Times.*"

"This is true?" Harper looked up to her best friend. She knew Nina would have already done her due diligence and checked the sources before she'd bring anything like this to her.

Nina nodded, confirming it. "And you've been named in the suit. In fact…" Harper knew she wasn't going to like what her friend was about to say. She squeezed her eyes shut and nodded, giving her permission to continue. "Trent has already issued a release saying it was all you and he didn't know anything about it."

Her eyes snapped open and she jumped to her feet. "He what?"

"I'm sorry, Harper. But the best defense is a strong offense. You need to call your lawyer right away and get on top of this."

"He planned it." She shook her head and wandered to the window, where she gazed out at the darkening sky. *The sun set earlier in the mountains.* It was a random thought, especially given everything else she had to worry about, but it was the one that stuck with her. "How could he do this…after everything…"

"Harper." Nina grabbed her arm and spun her around. "You need to focus."

Harper stared at her friend before she let her gaze drift over to Axel, who watch silently. "I can't call my lawyer," she said slowly. "He's Trent's lover."

As she spoke the words, the reality of her situation sunk in. Her gay husband, whom she'd shared a decade with as friends and business partners, had plotted and planned not only to leave her in a spectacular media frenzy, but also, and more painfully, was going to completely ruin her.

She wanted to crumple into a ball and cry. But more than that, she wanted to get back in that helicopter, fly down the mountain and hunt him and his weaselly boyfriend down until they both screamed for mercy.

"You can use mine."

Harper's head snapped up. "What did you say?"

"You'll use my lawyer." Axel repeated himself. "He's a good guy and one hell of a lawyer. I'll call him right now."

He walked away before she could protest. And even if she could, she wouldn't. She needed a lawyer, and he had one. It was turning out that Axel Jackson had a lot of things she wanted and more than a few that she needed.

CHAPTER FIVE

It was after nine by the time Harper got off the phone with his lawyer, John Kendrick. Axel had paced the main floor ever since she'd gone upstairs to talk to him. He was a good lawyer, and Axel had no doubt he'd help Harper and do a damn good job at it, but it didn't matter. His mate was in trouble and that made his bear crazy. The fact that she had no idea that she was his mate was beside the point. That would come in due time.

"I wrapped up your meals." Kade came out of the kitchen, a beer in his hand. "I figured you both would be hungry later."

Axel grunted a thank-you but didn't turn to look at his brother.

"You know, you could eat," Kade said. "You're not doing her any good out here driving us all crazy."

Axel spun around. "I fail to see how my concern for my—" He stopped himself and glanced at Nina, who was curled up in the corner of the couch, typing away on her laptop. "My guest," he amended but the slip had already been noticed by his brothers.

Luke swallowed the rest of his whisky in a gulp and crossed the room. "Let's get a drink, brother." It wasn't a suggestion and by the way Luke looked at him, he was not going to take no for an answer. Axel glanced up to the second story, where Harper's door was still closed.

"She'll be fine," Luke said.

He raised his eyebrows, but nodded slightly.

"We're just going to grab more drinks," Kade told Nina. "What can we bring you?"

Axel didn't stick around to listen to the answer. Instead, he bashed through the kitchen door, followed moments later by Luke and then Kade.

"Are you going to tell us what's going on with that woman?" It was Kade who asked as he grabbed a bottle of wine off the rack. "You almost ripped my head off earlier when I was talking to her and now you look like you're about to go all animal in the living room because she's upstairs on the phone."

"I should have ripped your head off," Axel growled. His blood ran hot and angry just thinking of the way his little brother had looked at Harper. That would never happen again. He'd make damn sure of it.

"What the hell, Axel?" Kade squared up and glared at him. "It's not like I was making out with her or anything and if I was—"

"He would have killed you," Luke finished. Kade stared at him, confused. "Because Axel seems to think our pretty blonde guest is his mate. Don't you, Axel?"

He couldn't deny it, so instead he went to the liquor cabinet, poured himself a shot of whisky and attempted to douse the fire inside him. It didn't work.

"Oh fuck." Kade groaned. "A mate? And a *human* mate at that? Perfect."

"If she *is* human," Luke muttered and they both turned to stare at him. Axel wanted to ask him what he meant by that, but he didn't have a chance before Kade was ranting again.

"You can't be serious."

Axel turned, refocused on his youngest brother. "Do you think I planned this?"

"Still." Kade shook his head. "Can you imagine what the old man will say?"

"I don't care." He poured himself another shot. "All I care about is having her."

"And what about what she wants?" Luke asked. "I can't imagine she wants anything to do with a bear."

"It won't matter." But Axel knew it did. At least a little. It would matter less once he claimed her. She'd still have a choice, of course, but once he had her... He tossed the second shot back.

"This is so messed up." Kade shook his head. It took all the restraint Axel had to keep from throwing his brother to the ground and asserting his dominance. *The kid was getting way too lippy for his own good.* And he might have done just that if the kitchen door hadn't swung open at that moment.

"Hey," Nina said. "I hope I'm not interrupting, but I thought maybe we could get another glass for that wine. Harper's on her way down and something tells me she's going to need a drink."

"Absolutely," Luke said. "We'll be right out."

Nina flashed a sexy smile and disappeared back into the living room.

Axel made a move to follow, but his brother's arm stopped him. "Are you going to be able to control yourself?"

He knew what Luke was really asking. He'd been there earlier when Axel's bear had tried to get out. He'd never before had trouble controlling his animal. Never. Of course, he'd never had the scent of his female filling his senses before. This was new. Very new. His instincts were definitely clouded. Axel nodded. He'd be fine.

"That's a damn good thing." Kade walked past them. "Because we can't screw this up, Axel." He turned and looked at both his brothers in turn. "Not for a female. We've got a good thing going on here and I'm not going to let it blow up just because you think you found your mate. I'm not going to lose everything. Not again and definitely not because of a mate."

He turned and left the kitchen so fast Axel didn't have a chance to stop him. And even if he had…

"Let him go," Luke said. "You know he's still sensitive about Kira. You know how he feels about the idea of mates."

Axel nodded. He knew all too well. Kade thought Kira had thrown everything away and ruined everyone's lives, all for a mate. Just like his mother had. He blamed the whole idea of mating on the destruction of their family. But Kade didn't know how it felt to have that special female's scent run hot through his blood. The taste of her on his tongue. How his whole body craved more. How it craved everything. Hell, Axel hadn't known either. Not until Harper.

"Thank you." Harper took the offered glass of wine from Kade's hands and swallowed half the contents in a single gulp. After that marathon call with Axel's lawyer, she needed it. Hell, she needed something a whole lot stronger than wine, but it would do for now.

"That good, huh?" Nina settled into the couch with her own glass but Harper couldn't sit. There was no way she could relax, not with her entire life on the line. Trent had gone too far this time.

She shook her head and swallowed the rest of the wine. "I can't believe he'd do this to me," she said. "I mean, after everything I did…it doesn't even matter. He's obviously been planning it for a while. And they seem to have things locked up pretty tight, but I think I'm in good hands with John Kendrick. He seems to know his stuff and he's going to do a bit of digging tomorrow. There's nothing else I can do tonight."

"So Axel's lawyer is going to be okay?" Nina asked. "Because if you want to go back to the city and get—"

"No." Harper shook her head. "That's the last thing I want. And John agrees. He thinks I should stay put and stay away from the media frenzy. No one knows I'm here right now, so it's probably for the best if I hang out for a bit."

"John knows what he's talking about."

Harper turned to see Axel in the doorway. Her entire body reacted to his presence and the memory of his lips on hers. It seemed like a million years ago now. What would have happened if they hadn't been interrupted? She knew exactly what would have happened and her body trembled at the thought.

"He does," she said softly. He didn't look as if he was going to move any closer to her, so Harper walked across the room toward him. "Thank you so much for setting that up for me."

Axel's eyes were intense and they held her, almost daring her to come closer. So she did.

"Anytime." He breathed the word and if she hadn't been standing so close, she wouldn't have heard it at all. There was so much implied in that one simple word that in an instant Harper's troubles melted away. She could have stared into his eyes all night. There was no doubt there was danger lurking in his gaze, but there was something else, too. Something that drew her in. "You'll stay here."

"Just for a bit," she said quickly.

"You'll stay for—"

"I'm not sure that's the best idea." It was Luke who spoke as he pushed his way between them. "I mean, of course, we want to help, Harper." He looked at her quickly before he returned his hard glare to his brother. "But we do have other guests scheduled later this week and—"

"She'll stay with me." Axel pushed him aside. His eyes never left hers. "I mean, she can stay in my cabin."

"And you'll stay where exactly?" Luke asked.

He focused on Harper for a moment before he turned to his brother. "With you." His words said one thing, but the look he'd given her said something entirely different.

A chill went through her but the damp heat that bloomed between her legs told her she was completely on board with that idea. No matter how ridiculous.

"Axel, I—"

"It's settled." He dismissed his brother and then seemed to remember himself and possibly his manners. "As long as you're okay with that."

She nodded. "Yes," was all she could manage.

It was crazy. But everything about the situation was crazy. From Trent, to the charges, to finding herself at a remote mountain lodge, to being completely under the spell of the most gorgeous man she'd ever laid eyes on. Crazy didn't come close to describing what was going on. Yet, Harper had never felt so sure about anything in her life.

"Harper, can I talk to you for a minute?" Nina didn't give her a chance to say no before she dragged her upstairs to her room. As soon as the door was shut, her friend turned on her. "What are you thinking? You can't stay with him."

She shrugged. "Why not? Besides, I'm not really staying *with* him. He's going to stay with his brother."

Nina gave her a look but Harper only shrugged, so Nina tried again. "You know, you could stay with me."

"I could, but that wouldn't be nearly as much fun, would it?"

"He's a…well…he's…"

"Weren't you the one who told me I deserved to have a little fun?"

Nina nodded.

"And weren't you the one who told me I needed to get laid?"

"Well…yes…"

"I'm pretty sure that will happen if I stay in his cabin." A rush of heat flowed through her as she spoke. Absolutely that would happen if she stayed with Axel and judging by the way her body reacted, she couldn't wait.

"I'm sure it will," Nina conceded. "It's just…you can't run away from your life."

"And I'm not." Not wanting to waste any more time, Harper packed the few items she'd bothered to unpack earlier. "We just got here. And I can't go back right now anyway. Not until John gives me the all-clear." She turned and looked at her best friend. "And frankly, even when he does tell me it's okay to go back, I'm not sure I'm going to want to."

"You've been here less than twenty-four hours. You can't be serious that you want to stay *here.*"

"Maybe not here." Harper shrugged. "But maybe." She shook her head and turned away. "I don't know. All I know is I don't know if I'm going to be in a hurry to go back to LA and that life. Because even when John does clear my name, and he will, there won't be anything left for me there. My reputation has already been destroyed. I won't be able to work. And even if I could..."

"You hate LA," Nina finished for her.

Harper nodded and sat on the edge of the mattress. "I do."

Nina wrapped her arm around Harper's shoulders and squeezed. "I know you do. Maybe it's for the best that everything happened."

Harper laughed. "Well, I'm sure it could have happened in a slightly different way and I would have been okay with that, too."

"Agreed." They shared a laugh and a hug. "So you're going to stay? With Axel?" Nina wiggled her eyebrows. "I guess I don't blame you," she continued. "He's yummy and I meant what I said earlier. You do deserve to have a little fun. Even if it's just temporary. Go for it, girl."

Harper smiled. With everything she was uncertain about, staying at Grizzly Ridge, at least for a little while, suddenly seemed like the best idea she'd heard in a long time. Especially if it involved a little *fun* with a mountain man like Axel.

CHAPTER SIX

It almost killed him, but Axel reluctantly agreed to wait until the following evening after dinner to move Harper's things to his cabin. He'd spent the majority of the day answering Nina's questions about the Ridge and trying to avoid Harper. Fortunately, Luke had taken her on another hike. Fortunate only in the sense that if Axel had even one second alone with the woman, he was fairly sure he would have pinned her hands over her head and kissed her until her legs would no longer hold her up. He needed her with a primal urge he'd never experienced before, and judging by the way she'd stared at him over the dinner table, she felt exactly the same way. It would be torture for him to take her into his cabin and not show her in graphic detail exactly what he'd fantasized about all day.

But he would.

Only if she wanted him to.

"I'm sorry the accommodations aren't ideal," he said as they walked out into the night air, toward his cabin. "It would be preferable to keep you in the main lodge, but with the big group coming tomorrow, I guess this is the only real solution."

He was lying through his teeth; having his mate in his cabin was absolutely the ideal solution. Axel also noted that neither of them mentioned the other, probably more practical solution of Harper staying in Nina's room. A solution that conveniently enough had never been brought up.

"It's fine." She flashed him a smile that made his crotch ache. Either she had no idea how sexy she was, or she did and took joy in torturing him.

In a desperate effort to get his mind off all the things he wanted to do with her mouth, Axel made another lame attempt at conversation. "I suppose you could have waited until morning to bring your things over. We didn't have to move you tonight." He had her suitcase under one arm, the other wrapped protectively around her shoulders as he led her through the dark to his cabin. Not that he'd wanted her to wait. It was exactly the opposite, in fact. He wanted—no, he needed—her as close as possible to him. Now that he'd found her, the bear in him was not going to let her go without a fight. It didn't matter that they'd just met. They were connected on a much deeper level and she knew it too, even if she didn't know what it was that she was feeling. Axel was sure of it. More than he'd ever been sure of anything in his life. And for the moment, that would have to be enough for both of them.

"There didn't seem to be much point," she said. He could tell she was trying to be brave, but the events of the last few days had definitely taken their toll. She looked exhausted and as much as Axel would have liked to show her a different way to relax, he was going to have to take his time. "Nina thinks I'm crazy for staying over here at all," she continued. "I mean, I don't even know you."

Axel stopped and put his free hand on her arm. "You already know everything you need to know." His eyes pierced hers and even in the dim light he could see her pupils react to his stare. "And anything else you want to know," he continued as he started to walk again, "all you have to do is ask."

"I plan on it."

He tried but failed not to smile at her bravado. She was definitely a feisty one. *Good.* She'd have to be to survive everything her ex was putting her through. The one thing that continued to bother Axel was how she could have let herself get into such a situation with a man. She was a strong woman; he could see that. So why had she let any man use her the way he had? She deserved more. So much more. And Axel was just the man to show her exactly what she deserved.

Harper hesitated as they stepped up to the porch and he opened the door to his cabin. Each of the brothers had built simple homes, and although they were all similar in a lot of ways, they were also very different. Axel's cabin consisted of two small rooms and an oversized bathroom that boasted both a double spray shower and an extra-large jetted tub. His brothers teased him about the bathroom, but he didn't care. There simply wasn't anything better than sinking into a tub full of steaming hot water after a hard run through the mountains.

Or at least he hadn't thought there'd be anything better. He stole a glance over to Harper next to him. He'd been wrong. Climbing into the bathtub with his mate would be infinitely better. But he was getting ahead of himself.

He flicked the light switch to illuminate the main room of the cabin. "After you."

She stepped into the room. It was comfortable, but fairly unadorned with a desk in one corner, a small dining set in the other, and two overstuffed chairs and a couch that faced a rock fireplace. Two large bookshelves lined one wall. Reading was another thing his brothers liked to tease him about, but he didn't care. It was his preferred way to spend the evenings.

At least it had been.

"Make yourself at home," he said. "The bedroom is right through here." Axel led the way through the door into the back bedroom. "It's not much, but you should find it comfortable enough." He tossed the suitcase on the king-sized bed and moved to the long low dresser against the wall. "I'll just empty a few drawers for you. I don't have much stuff any—"

"What about you?"

He froze and turned slowly at the question. "What about me?" She stood close. Really close. He inhaled deeply and filled his senses with the essence of her. She was all spice. She smelled like cinnamon and cloves, with just a hint of sweet apple. He'd never get tired of her scent. But there was something else, too. He closed his eyes and inhaled deeply, aware of how it must look to her.

"Where are you going to sleep?"

Axel opened his eyes to see her watching him. A smile played on her lips and she took a step closer. Her aroma intensified.

Arousal.

That was it. She was turned on. He'd caught a sniff of it a few times in the last few days, particularly the night before when they'd shared that kiss in the Den. But now it was different. It was intense. *How had he not recognized the scent earlier?*

That was easy. He'd never had his mate in front of him before. Let alone his mate standing in his bedroom. Turned on. His cock thickened in his jeans with the knowledge. Axel knew he should be the gentleman. He should excuse himself to sleep at Luke's. It shouldn't even be an option.

It wasn't an option. Except, with the way Harper looked at him, it was.

He took a step toward her to close the small gap between them and reached out to brush a strand of hair from her cheek. "That depends."

She tilted her head and lowered her lashes in a look that was both so innocent and dangerous at the same time, Axel's body vibrated from the effort of restraining himself.

"On what?" Her voice came out almost as a whisper, but there was no mistaking the strength behind the question.

He couldn't hold back. Not anymore. He had to have her.

"On, this." Axel wrapped one hand behind her head and pulled her into him. His lips met hers in a crush. He should be gentle, ease her into the kiss, but what he *should* do and what his bear *needed* to do were definitely not one and the same. A moan slipped from her lips and she pressed herself closer to him, until he could feel the heat of her soft, curvy body through his clothes. That was all the answer he needed.

Axel's other arm wrapped around her; his hand rested on her perfectly round ass. He grabbed on and spun her, walking her back toward the wall. He was careful to soften the blow as they hit the wall, but the moment he had her trapped between the logs and his body, he released her. His arms caged her in. He kissed her again. This time, his tongue found his way inside her mouth. It tangled with his as he explored the heat of her, tasted her spicy sweetness. He could get drunk on the taste of her, but he wanted more. Needed more.

He pulled back to look at her. Harper's chest heaved enticingly as she worked to regain her composure. His eyes lingered on the heavy, full breasts that strained against the cotton of her shirt. It would only take one quick move to release them. To have them in his hands. His mouth. With a groan, he forced his gaze upwards, to her lips red and swollen with passion, her blue eyes, dark with a need of her own.

"You didn't answer my question," she said after a moment, her eyes not leaving his.

Her whole body trembled from his kiss. She couldn't remember the last time she'd been kissed so thoroughly. Hell, she'd never been kissed like that. And she wanted more. But she also needed a moment to breathe. To pull together her thoughts. She waited for him to answer her question, both needing and dreading his answer. She didn't have to wait long.

Axel stepped forward and closed the tiny space she'd put between them. His eyes, normally so dark, held flashes of gold in them. She couldn't look away; they held her. His hand slipped up to her chin, cupping it possessively before sliding down to her neck. His touch sent chills racing through her and moisture pooled between her legs.

Axel's hand twisted through her hair and when he gently but firmly pulled it to one side to expose her neck to him, she thought her body might explode from the need building in her.

"Babe, nobody will be sleeping tonight," he growled before his mouth pressed to the sensitive skin beneath her ear and he worked his mouth along her neck. He held her firmly in one hand as his other gripped her hip to hold her up, which was a damn good thing because Harper could no longer trust her legs to support her.

Heat and hunger flowed through her as he nipped and sucked the skin on her neck. She knew he was marking her, but she didn't care and she couldn't have moved her head away from his strong grip if she wanted to.

And she didn't.

Harper had never moved so quickly with a man. Not that she'd had any opportunity to move any way with anybody in years. In fact, it had been so long since she'd been with a man, she was a little worried. *What if she didn't do it right? What if she forgot how?* Axel seemed so sure of himself, so…dominant. She'd be mortified if she screwed it up.

Axel's lips stilled on her neck and then he pulled away. She felt the absence of his mouth instantly. "What's wrong?"

Harper shook her head. "Nothing." She smiled in a way she hoped was seductive. "Absolutely nothing."

He didn't look as if he believed her, but his hands reached out and wrapped around her hips, squeezing the flesh there before slowly working their way up her sides. His fingers traced the swell of her breasts. "You're tense."

She shook her head, but when his fingers circled slowly over her nipple, it took her breath away. Through the thin fabric and lace of the bra, her nipple hardened and Axel made a sound of approval. "You need to stop thinking." His fingers still moved in slow, torturous circles. "Just let yourself feel." His fingers locked over her hard, throbbing nipple and pinched just hard enough to make her gasp and drive all thoughts from her head. "Better."

The delicious pulsing coursed from her nipple through her body until she could feel it in her core. And then his fingers were gone. Harper only had half a second to recover from the intensity before Axel's mouth locked over her breast, suckling her through the layers of her clothing. The feel of him was exquisite. She threw her head back, arching against him to give him better access.

"Axel...I..."

"Stop." He lifted his head from his task and stared at her. "Thinking."

He released her, almost causing her to stumble backward, but caught her quickly with both hands on the front of her t-shirt. In a move so quick she almost didn't see it, he tore through the cotton of her shirt, leaving it in shreds. Her bra hung from her arms as well, baring her heavy, heaving breasts to him.

"How did you—"

Her question was cut off with a firm pinch of her nipple while his mouth latched onto the other breast, giving it the attention it had been aching for. A mixture of pleasure and pain radiated through her and she writhed against him, desperate to press herself against his hard body.

"I like it better when you stop thinking," he said with a dangerous grin. "I like it so much I'm going to make sure you can't think of a damn thing tonight except for how good you feel."

Her body shuddered with the possibilities and she couldn't think of a good reason to object. Especially with the way he looked at her with hunger in his eyes.

* * *

He was moving too fast. Not for him, but for her. Every once in a while, he could see a flash of hesitation in her eyes. But he also saw desire. Need. A whole hell of a lot of need.

The logical part of his brain told him he needed to slow down and court her a little bit, but the bear inside him was not about to be tamed. He needed her and he hadn't realized just how much until she was in his cabin. The tiny space was full of her scent, heavy with desire. Harper needed him just as badly as he needed her. She just didn't know it yet. She was overthinking everything too damn much.

But that was about to change.

He squeezed his hands into the soft flesh at her hips. Just enough curves to sink his fingers into. She was perfect. With ease, Axel lifted her and just as he knew she would, Harper reflexively wrapped her legs around his waist.

"No," she protested. "Put me down. I'm too heavy."

"You're perfect." He dropped his face to her bare breasts and kissed and suckled them until the protests died on her lips. He knew exactly how to make her brain shut off so all she could focus on was feeling what she needed to feel and that's exactly what she was going to do. "But you have too many clothes on."

Without giving her a chance to protest, he kissed her hard and deep; he lifted her away from the wall and carried her the short distance to the bed, where he placed her softly on the quilt. His fingers traced the inner seam of her jeans to rest on her belt buckle. He locked eyes with her, giving her a chance to call it off. It was the only chance she'd have because if he thought he was hard to control right now, he'd be totally lost the second she was completely naked in front of him.

She nodded and her tongue darted out between her lips.

Axel growled as his cock pulsed hard in his jeans. He ripped the belt buckle free and tore her pants from her body.

Harper's eyes widened, but not in fear.

"How...what..."

"Later," was his only answer. "First." He knelt on the floor next to the bed and with his hands on her thighs, pulled her close with one tug. "This." He bent his head and licked her center. The sweet, spicy flavor of her burst on his tongue, and Axel had to concentrate to keep from losing control. Her body trembled with her need for him, and it only made him hungrier for her.

With both his hands, he held her deliciously muscular thighs open and ravished her with his tongue until he could feel the telltale quiver in her body. She was close. So close. He wanted to give her everything. Over and over again. Without hesitation, he slipped first one and then two fingers inside her while his tongue circled and flicked her hard clit. Seconds later, her body tensed as she arched her back and cried her release, but still he didn't relent his attentions on her body.

Harper moaned and squirmed under him. She was perfect. Responsive, gorgeous, and all his. His mate. He knew it in every fiber of his body. His bear was so close to the surface, he needed to hold back to keep from frightening her. But as he kissed his way up her body, focusing on the soft flesh at her waist—*So wonderfully curvy and sexy. His*—he knew she felt it too. The only difference was Harper couldn't know what it meant. She was not a bear.

Or was she? His instincts were muddled, but there was something about her scent he couldn't quite place.

It complicated things.

He couldn't focus on that right now.

"Axel, I...I need you."

She didn't have to ask him twice. Lightning fast, he picked her up and dropped her back softly on the bed before he reached into the nightstand drawer to find a condom. He sheathed himself before he poised himself at her entrance. He paused. There would be no turning back. At least for him. Once he was with her, he'd be lost. She'd be his forever. Even without claiming her. He knew it. And if she didn't feel the same way…if she didn't love him and accept him…he'd be alone.

Axel knew enough about how fated mates worked. He'd never experienced it, and if it hadn't been for his sister Kira and her mate and seeing their love for himself, he never would have believed it. What he did know was he'd have to hold himself back from the act of mating her. For now. He'd keep it only to sex.

Only sex?

The idea was laughable because Axel knew the moment he was inside her, he'd need more. But he couldn't have her. Not as a mate. Not yet.

It was a risk.

He should wait. Be certain.

Axel looked down at the woman beneath him: Her blonde hair splayed over the pillow. Her heavy, full breasts with their peaked, firm nipples begged for his mouth on them. Her lush, curvy body that was made for his… *There was no waiting.*

He bent and took her mouth in his, making love with his tongue as he entered her. Harper gasped; her body tensed as she adjusted to him and when he felt her relax once more, he lifted his head. She was tight and hot and…

"Damn, you feel so fucking good."

Her lips curled up and she grinned wickedly. Axel thrust deep and her face transformed with passion. Watching her pleasure play out all over her face as his body rocked with hers was the sexiest thing he'd ever seen.

Mine.

His bear growled as he rocketed toward release but he held back.

As if Harper could feel he was holding back, she wrapped her legs around him and squeezed, pulling him even closer to her.

Damn, this woman.

He made the rules; he set the pace. But with Harper, all bets were off and damned if it wasn't the hottest thing he'd ever experienced. Axel picked up the pace and the intensity of his thrusts; Harper groaned her pleasure as her fingernails raked down his back.

It wasn't long before he felt her body tense with her impending orgasm. He reached between them and pressed just enough on her clit as their bodies joined together to send them together into a desperate, intense release.

As his body shook and vibrated over hers, there was only one thought going through his head.

My mate. Mine.

Never before had Harper experienced sex like that. Hell, she didn't even know sex could be like that. What had she been missing all those years with Trent? Or not really *with* Trent, but being loyal to Trent. Regardless, now that her eyes had been opened to what could be, she was never going back to mediocre sex. Or worse, celibacy.

Harper shuddered with the thought.

"Are you cold?"

Axel pulled her closer so her back was pressed up against the hard length of his body. She shook her head. "How could I be?" she murmured. "You're like a furnace."

In response, he pulled her tighter. "I sure know how to heat you up," he teased.

"You do." Harper wiggled her bum and felt the instant response in his body. "You're not the only one with those skills."

He kissed her hair with such tenderness that Harper felt something spark deep inside. It had been amazing sex, as she knew it would be. From the moment she laid eyes on Axel, she'd known he'd be an animal in bed and there was an attraction between them that couldn't be denied, and hadn't been. But there was something else between them, too. She couldn't quite put her finger on it, and that concerned her.

When Axel kissed the back of her neck and bare shoulders, any concern she had melted away and headed directly to her core, and the insatiable need she seemed to have for the man. A need that had grown quickly and only seemed to be growing stronger.

She pushed any thoughts that would distract her from the task at hand out of her mind and rolled over so she could press her breasts up against his hard chest and kiss him properly.

CHAPTER SEVEN

"Good morning."

Nina looked up from her iPad and tilted her head to examine Harper as she walked into the kitchen in the Den.

"Judging by that look on your face, I'd say it was a pretty damn good night, too." She winked and shook her head but in the next breath said, "Tell me everything. Is he as good in bed as he looks?"

Harper opened her mouth to answer, but her friend cut her off. "No," she said. "You don't even need to answer that. I can tell. He was better."

"Oh yes," she agreed. Harper poured herself a cup of coffee from the carafe in front of Nina. "So much better than you could even imagine." She wasn't one to kiss and tell, but then again she'd never had anything worth telling before. Now that she'd just spent an intense night with some of the most toe-curling orgasms of her life and an even more spectacular early morning, she had plenty to tell. More than that, she wanted to tell Nina. She sank into the chair next to her friend. "I have never—"

"Never what?" Kade interrupted them as he walked out of the pantry with a bowl. He winked at Harper with eyes so much like his brother's it was slightly unsettling. "Never mind. You don't need to answer that. I think I have a pretty good idea of what you're talking about."

A blush burned up Harper's neck. Of course, everyone at the Ridge would know exactly what had gone on in Axel's cabin. She shrugged. It didn't matter. Not really. She was having fun. Letting herself go and enjoying herself the way she should have years ago. She was a modern woman with needs and a mind of her own. She could do whatever the hell she wanted to do, and damned if she didn't want to keep doing Axel.

Well, if everyone already knew what she'd done and planned on continuing to do, she was going to own it. Gone were the days of Harper allowing others to tell her how to present herself in public. It was long past time she made the decisions about how she was going to live her life. She tossed her hair over her shoulders and sat up tall. "If you think I'm talking about getting busy with that sexy big brother of yours, you'd be right."

"That's what it was?"

Harper froze at the voice and turned to see Axel, his broad shoulders framed in the doorway, the anger that vibrated from his body only barely contained.

"Axel. I—"

"You were just telling everyone how we'd been *getting busy*." His words were hard and cold.

Was he seriously getting upset at her for saying what everyone already knew? Sure, maybe she shouldn't have said anything at all, but he had no right to get upset with her. She sat straighter and squared off her shoulders to him. "So what if I was?"

A noise that sounded suspiciously like a growl came from him and his fist hit the doorframe with such force that Harper felt it across the room, but she didn't back down.

"Axel," Kade interjected. "We were just fooling around. Talking about—"

"Getting busy." He repeated the words again, not taking his eyes off hers. This time when he said them, Harper could see hurt in his gaze as well as anger. *Could he really be upset that she'd made light of their night together?*

"Axel." She left her coffee untouched and rose from her seat. If it had been any other man standing there looking as though he barely had a handle on his anger, she might have been scared. But it was Axel. They may have only had one night together, but it was enough for her to know that there was nothing to be scared of.

Except for wanting another night.

She pushed the thought away and crossed the room to him. He stood unmovable, an impenetrable wall. When she reached out to him and touched his chest softly with her fingertips, the spark of energy that flew from his body into hers almost knocked her backward. *What was it about touching this man?* But she didn't withdraw her hand. Instead, she pressed her palm to his hard muscles. "I didn't mean anything by—"

"Well, there's the happy couple." Together, Axel and Harper turned to see Luke come in through the back door. "I'm surprised to see the two of you before noon."

"There's coffee, here," Harper replied with a quick smile, desperate to defuse the situation.

"That's it." Axel jerked back from Harper's touch and instead of going after his brother the way she might have expected, he stepped backward and with impressive speed, moved through the main room and out the front door.

"Axel!" Without thinking, Harper ran after him. Something she couldn't explain drew her to him. But he was a lot faster than her, and by the time she got out to the large front porch, he'd disappeared. "Axel!" she called again.

"Stupid man," she muttered to herself. She couldn't figure out why she cared so deeply after only one night, but she did. There were probably a million things she should have been doing, like checking in with the lawyer to see whether her career had been further destroyed overnight. Or maybe she should have been on the phone trying to minimize the damage that was no doubt being done to her reputation in her absence, but none of those things were important. Not when she knew Axel was upset with her. With a sigh of frustration, Harper ran down the stairs and headed into the woods in search of the man who was beginning to affect her in more ways than one.

He needed to get away from her before his bear lost his control. *What was happening to him?* He never lost control. He was the level-headed one. He was the one who kept it all together. *He* was the one who was completely unaffected by females.

Until now.

Dammit.

Axel ran hard into the woods. The need to shift into his bear and run along the ridge until the feelings that were barely under the surface were exhausted and gone was strong. It's what he should have done the night before instead of taking the damn woman to his cabin. What had he been thinking?

He hadn't.

He'd been going on pure instinct. And his instinct had said he needed to have her. His mate. No matter what the cost. And there would be a cost. How could there not be? The Jackson clan didn't mate frivolously. They didn't believe in it. Every match had to be thought out. Strategic for the survival of their lineage. It was why Kira had been cast out. As an alpha female, she'd been crucial to the lineage of the clan. But she'd chosen an unacceptable mate. Or, the way she told it, fate had chosen him.

No. Axel didn't believe in mates, or fated mates. *Especially* human fated mates. *No.* He shook his head to clear his head of thoughts of Harper, naked on his bed, her beautiful body pressed to his. *It couldn't happen.* Nothing about them together should have happened. Unless it was meant to be a fling. One night of meaningless passion. Except it wasn't.

Not to him.

Axel's bear roared, threatening to escape.

But that's all it had been to Harper. He'd heard her in the kitchen when she thought he wasn't there, and then again, her flippant remark to Luke right in front of him. Their night together had meant nothing to her.

That's what he ran from. What he needed to escape.

His muscles bunched and tensed, ready to shift into the animal that would allow him the release his mind so desperately craved.

"Axel!"

The voice split the air, reaching him through the trees, followed moments later by her scent. She was in the woods. Axel slowed his pace, his ears tuned, listening for her.

"Axel," she called again. "Where are you?"

There was a slight tremor to her voice. *Was she scared?* His instincts took over. No matter how she felt about him, he could not, would not stand for her to be hurt or scared in any capacity. He spun on his heel and took off in the opposite direction, directly for her. For his mate.

The forest was more confusing than she'd thought. There were no paths leading her to Axel. Not that she expected there to be, but part of her expected him to appear the moment she set foot into the trees. But it all started to look the same. Harper stopped walking and turned slowly, trying to get her bearings.

"Axel?" She called again, but she sounded less and less sure of herself, even to her own ears. "Where are you, you stupid man?" she muttered to herself and stomped off in a different direction. A move she immediately regretted as her foot landed in a hole of some kind and she crumpled to the ground in a heap. Pain radiated through her leg.

"Ow!" Harper squirmed on the ground and muttered a curse of expletives as she extracted her foot from the hole.

"That wasn't very lady-like."

Her head snapped up to see Axel leaning nonchalantly against a tree trunk, as if he'd been there the entire time. He had a little grin on his face, but she could still see the hard press of his jawline that told her he was still upset. But she'd be dammed if she could figure out what he was so upset about.

"It wasn't supposed to be lady-like," she retorted. She pulled herself up and crossed her bad leg up over the other so she could take off her shoe. Her ankle throbbed something fierce and she was positive it was already swelling up inside her boot. "It hurts. A lot. I think I broke it."

"You shouldn't take that—"

She pulled her boot off, the pressure instantly relieved.

"Off," he finished lamely.

"Why shouldn't I?" She stretched her leg. The pain was still present, but at least it wasn't pressing down on her foot so intently anymore. "It feels so much better."

"The swelling will be out of control." Axel bent down in front of her, and took her foot in his hands. His large hands were surprisingly gentle. It shouldn't have been surprising, really, considering the care and attention he'd given her the night before. But that was different. "We'll never get the boot back on," he said thoughtfully as his fingers gently prodded her flesh.

"Ow!" She tried to pull her foot back in reflex but he held firm; his fingers started smooth, gentle circles over her sock.

"I don't think we'd get it back on anyway. It's pretty swollen already. Does this hurt?"

"Ow!"

"Can you move your ankle?"

She tried and instantly shook her head. "No."

He looked up at her and she could see the genuine concern in his eyes. This man was increasingly difficult to figure out. "I hope a sprain is all it is," he said. "But if it hurts all the way up your leg, you might have broken it."

She had to look away from his intense gaze. "I'll be fine." Harper slid her foot away from him and attempted to stand, but the pain that shot through her foot and up her leg threatened to drop her to the ground. She gritted her teeth, but the groan escaped anyway.

Axel was on his feet, his arms around her in a flash.

"Don't try to stand. I just told you, it's likely broken."

"It's fine."

He shook his head and growled. "Stubborn woman. It's *not* fine."

She felt tiny in his embrace, he encircled her so completely. Despite herself, and the frustration she'd felt for him only moments ago, a coil of heat flared up in her core at his closeness. Damn, she wanted him again. Always.

"Maybe we could just sit for a minute." She managed to get the words out, despite the flurry of feelings that roiled through her. "It should be okay in a little bit."

He shook his head, but released her and helped her sit again. He moved a short distance away and sat on a log facing her. They stared at each other for a moment, each waiting for the other to speak first. Finally, Axel broke the silence. "What were you thinking, wandering through the woods like that? You could have gotten lost."

"But I didn't." She raised her chin defiantly.

"You would have if I hadn't come to find you."

She pressed her lips into a hard line. "That's not true. You didn't have to *find* me."

"You're right." His grin was mischievous and dammed if it didn't do all kinds of things to her insides. "All I had to do was follow your scent."

Scent? Of all the things to say, that was definitely the oddest. Her confusion must have shown on her face because Axel quickly modified, "I meant, your voice. You're very loud, you know. Easy to find in the woods."

"Well, that's a good thing, right?" She crossed her arms over her chest. Mostly to keep them from shaking at his closeness, but if it made her look tough, that was an added bonus. "Being loud, I mean," she continued. "You know, to keep the animals away. It obviously worked."

He grinned again, and Harper could see the flash of desire in his eyes. "Almost," he said.

"Almost?"

"You kept them all away but one."

Heat rushed through her and settled in a pool of moisture between her legs. Her body screamed at her to forget all the confusion from earlier and just go with her original plan of having fun with him. But she couldn't. "Why did you take off like that?"

Axel recoiled as if she'd slapped him. He didn't even pretend not to know what she was talking about. "I needed some space."

"From me?"

"From everything."

"You were mad at me," she said. "At what I said to your brothers."

He nodded.

"That's not fair. I didn't say anything wrong."

"Yes, you did." His voice was deep, each word almost a growl. "You made light of what happened between us." His brown eyes darkened with intensity. "And there was nothing light about what happened."

Harper didn't know whether it was his choice of words or the way he looked at her with so much want and…possessiveness…but her body came alive under his scrutiny. He was absolutely right; there was nothing light about what went down between them. She'd been trying to ignore it, but with him right there, the way he stared at her…she couldn't.

And when he got up, crossed the distance between them and lifted her from her seat, being careful to hold her so she wouldn't put weight on her foot, she was instantly lost in him.

With one arm wrapped around her, supporting her body against his, Axel's other hand cradled her face. "I know you feel it, too," he said, his voice a rough whisper.
All she could do was nod in response. She didn't know what she was feeling, but it was definitely something.

"Say it."
"Say what?"
In answer, his mouth covered hers; his tongue plunged into her mouth, tasting the sweetness he'd craved since letting her out of his bed that morning. He never should have let her leave. Never should have let her go into the Den and make out like what they'd shared had been anything less than a perfect union of mates. She didn't know it yet, but she was his. Utterly, undeniably his. Every nerve in his body felt it.
He pulled away from her, sucking on her lower lip and leaving it swollen and sexy as hell when she looked up at him with shuttered eyes so heavy with passion she could barely think straight. "Say what you're feeling," he commanded.
Harper shook her head from side to side. "But I don't...I can't..."
"You can." He held her chin in one hand, holding her still, forcing her to look at him. "I know you feel it. I can sense it with my body." Her eyes flashed with something. A spark of acknowledgment, maybe. But still, Harper was confused. Of course she was. Hell, he was, too. But the more he thought of it, the more he knew it was true. But Harper had no idea what was happening to her, what Axel suspected she was. If she was his mate, the way he *knew* she was, then Harper had to have some bear in her

bloodline. It was probably such a small part of who she was that she likely had no idea. Which was why she couldn't explain or understand the feelings she had toward him. The undeniable pull toward him.

"Axel. I don't know what you want me to say. I...being with you..." Her voice was small, confused, almost scared. He couldn't stand seeing his strong mate so conflicted. "Well, it's been fun being with you. But that's all it is." Her words hit him in the heart. "It can never be anything more," she continued. "I'm worried you think there can be more with us, and as much as I..."

He stopped listening. He'd heard all he needed to in order to know there was no choice. He was going to have to tell her the truth. He was going to have to show her his bear. Help her to understand so she could come into her own and never be uncertain again.

"Harper, stop." He interrupted her. "I need to show you something." He set her down again, feeling the loss of her in his arms the second she was gone. "And I want you to promise that you won't get scared or freak out."

She shook her head. "You're scaring me right now. Axel...what's going on?"

"I promise, there's nothing to be scared of, but it will seem odd. At least at first. But it will help you understand a few things."

"What things?"

"How you're feeling." He pinned her with his eyes and she settled instantly, the way he knew she would. "Because I know you don't mean what you just said."

"Axel, I—"

"How you feel you could give up everything to be here with me after knowing me for such a short time." He ignored her protests and pushed on. The way she blinked and shook her head slightly told him she'd been thinking exactly that. "How you feel that you need to be with me. Close to me. Touching me, or you feel like you might die."

"That's extreme. I—"

"You feel it, don't you?"

She didn't answer, but pressed her lips together instead. "The reason you're feeling the way you are is because there's something more inside of you. Just like me. I'm not an ordinary man."

"Well, I knew—"

"No." He tried not to smile. He needed to stay focused. "I have an animal inside me, and I think you do, too. That's why you're feeling so drawn to me. We're mates."

"Mates?" She half scoffed, half laughed. "Like as in...mates-mates? That's the most ridiculous thing I've ever—"

He dropped to his knees in front of her and tried to take her hand. "Listen to me, Harper. It's not ridiculous. I've known my whole life, but for you...well, it's new. It's—"

"It's ridiculous, is what it is." She pushed him away and tried to stand but he promptly pushed her down, gently but firmly.

"Sit," he ordered. "Just let me show you." Before she could protest further, Axel turned and ran a slight distance into the woods. If she wouldn't listen to him, she'd just have to see it with her own eyes.

CHAPTER EIGHT

He was being ridiculous. *Mates?* That didn't even make sense. Sure, she was having feelings she'd never had before. But they were probably just a result of having the best sex of her life after way too long suppressed in a terrible marriage. And combined with the stress of her entire life collapsing around her…well, of course, she was feeling things she couldn't explain. But *mates?* What did that even mean?

Harper glanced around the small clearing she was in. They truly were in the middle of nowhere and she had no idea how to find her way back to the main lodge on her own. She stared in the direction he'd just disappeared and called after him. *Certainly he wouldn't leave her there on her own?* Especially not with a sore foot. But she couldn't figure out what he would do. She couldn't make sense of anything.

Everything was a mess. He was talking crazy about feelings and what was going on with her. But the craziest part wasn't what he'd said. It was that he was right. Every single thing he said about what she was feeling was spot on. Too bad it only made her more confused.

"Axel?"

She tried again to see whether she could spot him, but

there was nothing. And then, a shift of the branches, a rustling and…the biggest grizzly bear she'd ever seen—not that she'd ever seen one close up before—appeared in the small clearing.

Harper's first thought when the huge animal appeared was how beautiful an animal it was. She'd never seen a bear without the safety of distance between them before and this one was magnificent: dark fur that was so black it almost sparkled in the sun, a strong broad back, and dark eyes that were somehow familiar and not at all threatening.

Despite the lack of menace from the bear, Harper's second thought after processing that there was a giant and very dangerous animal standing only feet away from her was one of sheer panic. She instinctively tried to scoot backward, but fell off the log, her legs in the air. She scrambled to her feet and immediately sank to the ground again as the pain reminded her why she wasn't standing.

"Axel!" Harper screamed as the bear advanced slowly. He didn't look menacing or dangerous the way she assumed bears would. In fact, there was something very familiar about him but that didn't comfort her when the bear approached. She couldn't get away; there was no way she could escape. *She needed Axel and…* The thought hit her hard and fast.

The bear approached. Close enough she could feel his warm breath and look into his dark eyes. The eyes that were so familiar she could have sworn they were… *No. It wasn't possible.*

"Axel?" She breathed his name in a puff of air. Her heart seemed to freeze in her chest. The idea that Axel stood in front of her as a bear was too ludicrous to process, yet…

She was only just beginning to allow herself to think about the possibilities when the bear raised his head and lowered it, nodding in response to her question.

It was too much. Harper's last thought before she passed out was, *This can't be my life.*

Axel shifted the weight of her in his arms and snuggled her closer to his chest. He'd expected a variety of responses when he'd shown Harper his bear, but he hadn't expected her to pass out. Not really. But it was fine by him, because it meant he got to hold her close without any objections as he carried her back through the forest to the Den.

And there would be objections. His female was a feisty one, and there was no way she was going to accept the whole bear shifter thing without a fight. That much he knew.

Axel smiled to himself and pressed his lips to the top of her head as he broke through the tree line into the clearing. People milled about, and a few trucks he didn't recognize sat out front of the Den. Their guests had arrived early. Oh well, his brothers were more than capable of handling things. His only priority was Harper and staying by her side until she woke so he could explain everything.

"Where have you been?" Nina spotted them and ran across the field toward them, cutting Axel off before he could take the small path to his cabin. "I was worried—what happened? Is she okay? Harper?" Nina moved to touch her friend's forehead, but Axel turned deftly and kept her out of reach.

"She's fine. She had a little scare in the woods, but she'll be fine."

"A scare?" It was Luke who asked, his eyebrow raised. "What kind of scare?" From his tone, Luke already knew full well what had scared her.

"She needs to rest." Axel tried to push past them to get her to the cabin before she woke.

"Go settle her and come right back here," Luke said.

"I'm sure you can handle our guests for a few hours, Luke."

"It's not just the guests." Something in his brother's voice caught his attention, and Axel turned to hear the rest of what Luke had to say. "We have…visitors." He gestured with his head in the direction of the woods to the east. *The wolves.* They ran the ranch in the valley that was in direct competition with Grizzly Ridge; at least, that's how the wolf shifters saw it. As far as the Jackson brothers were concerned, they offered different things and they should all be able to work together. Too bad the wolves didn't see it that way. Axel had hoped to avoid any trouble with them for a little longer. "Maybe Nina can sit with her?" Luke suggested.

"Of course I can," Nina said quickly. "You guys take care of whatever you need to. You have a business to run. We'll be fine."

The last thing Axel wanted to do was leave Harper alone after what he'd just revealed to her. He needed to be with her when she woke to hold her and reassure her that she wasn't going crazy. But there was something in Luke's expression. He was worried about something and it no doubt had to do with whatever trouble the wolves were stirring up. He looked down to Harper's face, peaceful and beautiful in rest. She'd be awake soon. He looked back to Nina. *Maybe being with her friend might help. It could be grounding for her.*

And judging by the way Luke tensed next to him, he didn't have much of a choice. "Okay." He nodded. "Let me go settle her in the cabin. I'll be right there."

Luke nodded his agreement and without waiting to see

whether Nina would follow, Axel made his way up the path.

Only moments later, Axel had Harper tucked into his bed with strict instructions to her friend not to let her leave the cabin until he returned. He had to trust that she'd obey him, even though every instinct he had fought with him to stay with his mate and keep her safe. As the alpha of Grizzly Ridge, he had no choice. Something was not right, and he needed to figure out what it was.

He ran into Luke on the trail, waiting for him.

"What's going on?" he asked without preamble. "Is it the wolves? What's going on?"

"First tell me what happened back there."

Axel froze and stared at his little brother, who was hardly even half an inch shorter than him, and at six two not little by any stretch of the imagination. "What are you talking about?"

"Your female." It was the first time Luke had acknowledged that Harper was in fact his female. "What happened?"

There was no point in lying or drawing things out. "I showed her my bear."

Axel expected his brother to be surprised. Angry even. Instead, he dropped his head and shook it slowly. "No wonder she passed out."

"I had to do it."

"No." He raised his head and looked his older brother in the eyes in a way that almost made Axel assert his alpha. "You didn't," he continued. "She's a city girl with no idea what it's like out here with a guy like you. She's here on a holiday, Axel. That's it."

"That's not it." He crossed his arms over his chest. "She's my mate. We're fated."

"You're full of shit. There's no such thing."

Of course Luke didn't believe. Hell, Axel hadn't believed either. Not until it happened to him. Not until Harper. He'd suspected the idea of it might be true after Kira had run off, but suspecting something and experiencing it were two different things. Two *very* different things. "There is." He wouldn't fight with his brother. Not now. He knew from experience what a futile exercise it was. But he also wasn't about to back down. "And she's mine."

Luke opened his mouth as if he was going to argue with Axel some more, but he shook his head and ran his hands through his blond hair before changing tack. "We'll talk about it later," he said. "Right now we have bigger problems." He pointed to the trucks parked out front. "Our guests are here."

Axel nodded. "And?"

"Wolves," Luke confirmed. "Well, not wolves so much as visitors from their ranch."

Axel waved his hand, impatient for more details.

"They're from the city. California, actually." Luke raised an eyebrow.

Axel's hackles rose. "California?" He glanced back to where he'd left his female in the cabin. "We're getting a lot of that lately."

"That's what I thought." Luke walked back to the Den and Axel followed, reluctantly leaving Harper behind. "They're staying at Blackwood Ranch with the wolves, but apparently wanted to check us out, too. Kade set the New Yorkers up with some refreshments and I'll take them out for a hike as soon as they're settled in. But I thought you'd want to know about these two, especially considering they came from Blackwood."

Axel met his brother's skeptical look. Luke was right. He did want to know. Despite his efforts to be friends with the Blackwood wolves, including booking their entire group of New Yorkers on a trail ride the next day, they'd done their best to make it clear they weren't going to be friends. It seemed more than a little off that any guests of theirs would set foot on Grizzly Ridge.

When they reached the front porch of the Den, the two new arrivals were standing on the steps. One snapped pictures with a large camera while the other muttered into a recording device. When the men saw Axel and Luke, the one with the camera began to take pictures of them while the other man, a smaller, fancy dressed man stepped down off the price and extended his hand.

Axel shot a look at his brother. "Reporters? We already have a reporter." His instincts had kicked into overdrive. Something wasn't right about these two. Reluctantly, he shook the man's hand.

"Kevin Carr," the man said. "Reporter for Getting Around. And this is my photographer, Bruce Bonnet. We're excited to be here at the ranch to see—"

"The Ridge," Axel corrected. He pulled his hand back and stuffed it into his back pocket. "Grizzly Ridge. Where are you from again?"

"Getting Around," Kevin repeated. "It's a new travel website and we're excited to get in on the ground floor. It hasn't launched yet. We're still building content. We were scheduled in at Blackwood, but when we found out about Grizzly Ridge," he emphasized the *Ridge*, "we just knew it would be a great addition to the site and a huge benefit to you and your new business."

Axel crossed his arms and stared them down. He didn't like them. Something wasn't right about the pair, and although he couldn't put his finger on it, his bear was roaring to make them leave. "You should go back to the ranch. We're full."

"Axel." Luke grabbed his arm. "Can I talk to you for a minute?"

Begrudgingly, Axel allowed Luke to lead him a few feet away, but he didn't take his eyes off the men.

"I don't think we should reject them out of hand," Luke said.

"I don't like them."

"But it could be a good opportunity," his brother argued. "You said yourself we need as much exposure as we could get."

"Not from them. Besides, we don't have any room."

"It wouldn't hurt to answer some questions. They don't have to stay."

"I don't trust them." Axel didn't know whether it was something about the men, or the fact that his mate was sleeping not far away, unprotected and vulnerable after what she'd just seen. He'd never had to consider a mate before. It was an entirely new feeling to want to protect someone else. "It doesn't matter anyway; we have Nina. She's writing a piece."

"So, what if we ask her if she's heard of these guys?"

Axel shook his head.

"We'll keep an eye on them and make sure they're on the up-and-up." Axel turned to look at his brother. "We'll make it work."

He stared at Luke for a moment. His brother's instincts were clearly not affected by the men. *Maybe he was clouded by his female? Perhaps he wasn't able to think as clearly as he used to?* Reluctantly, Axel nodded. "Fine. They can stay for the day. But if anything—"

"Nothing will happen. And I'll go talk to Nina as soon

as I can to find out what she knows about these guys. In the meantime, why don't you figure out what you're going to do with the little situation you've created? I'm willing to bet she needs a little space to figure things out."

"What she needs is me." Axel clenched his hands into fists at his sides. It was all he could do to not turn and run back up to the cabin where Harper was no doubt awake by now.

"Brother." Luke clamped a hand on his shoulder and Axel reluctantly turned to look at him. "She's with her friend. Females need their friends. Give her some time."

He didn't like it. Every fiber in his body strained to be at her side, but on some level, Axel knew Luke was right. He'd give her some time to process what had happened in the woods.

But not too much. She had to understand. He *needed* her to understand.

CHAPTER NINE

It took Harper a moment to register where she was when her eyes opened. A moment later, she was frantically trying to scramble out of Axel's bed. Until the pain from her ankle shot through her.

"OW."

"Harper? Are you awake?"

She propped herself up on her elbow and looked around Axel's small cabin. "Nina?"

"I'm in the bathroom. Hold on." A second later, a flush was followed by the sound of the sink and then, finally, mercifully, Nina.

Her friend was at her side, hand in hers, and Harper had never been so happy to see her friend in her life. "Thank goodness it's you."

"Of course it's me. I'm here." Nina patted her hand. "Axel said you had quite the fall in the woods. How do you feel?"

"Axel?" Harper looked around again. She couldn't see him. "Is he here?"

Nina shook her head and scooted up on the bed.

Conflicted feelings rolled through her. She wanted him there by her side, but at the same time, she wanted him far away from her. And she couldn't figure out why. Her hand went to her head and she rubbed the side of it. It wasn't sore. Nina said she'd fallen. *Did she hit her head?*

"Is your head okay? Do you need something?"

"No." Harper shook her head once and blinked hard. "It's fine. But I have the strangest feeling that I'm forgetting something. Something about Axel... Something that happened."

"You must have hit your head." Nina poured her a glass of water from the jug on the bedside table and handed it to her.

"No." Harper took a sip. "That's not it." Her memory was right on the tip of her consciousness; she just couldn't quite reach it. She'd been in the woods with Axel. She'd chased him in there and gotten lost. But he'd found her. He'd declared his love for her, kissed her—oh, she remembered that kiss—he'd told her they were meant to be together, that they were—

"Axel will be back soon, I suspect," Nina said, breaking Harper's line of thinking. "He didn't want to leave you, but Luke told him it was important and made him go. It was crazy," she continued. "He was like a protective animal over—"

"Animal?" The hair on the back of Harper's neck stood up. *That was it.* He'd said they were mates. *Mates.* It was ridiculous. It was animalistic. And then there'd been a bear. "A bear." She whispered the words, but Nina heard.

"Well, I don't know if I'd say it was like a bear, so much as a—"

"A bear." Harper sat up as her mind went a million miles an hour. *Axel had been a bear. He was gone and then...the bear and...*

"Okay." Nina jumped up off the bed. "If you say so. Speaking of Axel, I should probably tell him you're awake.

Like I said, he was pretty worried. Hey." Nina stopped and came back to the bed. "Are you okay? You don't look good. You look like you saw a—"

"A bear."

"I was going to say a ghost, but if you insist on this bear thing." She shook her head. "Hey, I was thinking that maybe I'd stay up here with you for a few more days. I don't feel right leaving you with all the legal bullshit that Trent's putting you through. It's a good time for you to have a friend nearby."

Harper was only half listening. "Of course," she said.

"You want me to stay?"

"Why wouldn't I? But don't you have an article to write?"

Nina tossed her hair over her shoulder proudly. "Already done. And submitted, too. I was inspired by this place. It's amazing. I got it done early. Way ahead of deadline. And I even talked my editor into letting me post a teaser on the website. It was up late last night. Soon, the whole world will know about Grizzly Ridge. In fact, it seems that word is already getting out. The New Yorkers showed up early along with a few new guests who didn't have any reservations while you guys were in the woods. I think that's what Axel is dealing with right now."

Harper nodded absentmindedly. "Nina? Do you believe in love at first sight?"

"What?"

"I mean…" She searched her brain for the right words. "Do you believe in people being fated for each other? Like a destiny?"

Nina dropped heavily onto the bed, no longer interested in finding Axel to tell him Harper was awake. "Are you talking about you and Axel? Because he's super yummy and all and you know I wanted you to have a little fun and get it out of your system. I mean, Lord knows you deserve to sow some wild oats or any oats really after being married for so long to Trent, but love at first sight? Harper...that's crazy. You've only known each other a few days. You can't seriously be thinking of—"

"I don't know what I'm thinking." She shook her head and forced a smile. "But you're right. It's all a little crazy."

"It's the sex, right?" Nina nodded knowingly. "If you've gone too long without good sex, it can be emotional when you finally do have it. Maybe you're just feeling something more than you should be because you finally had an orgasm. I'm assuming you had an orgasm..."

Harper nodded and her smile widened.

"I knew it!" Nina bounced on the bed. "Tell me everything. I want all the details. Don't leave anything out."

"I thought you were going to go get Axel."

Nina waved a hand, dismissing her. "He can wait. I can't. Now spill."

Axel still didn't have a good feeling about the two new arrivals, but Luke was probably right. The likelihood of there being an actual problem with the men was slim. Especially if they stayed only for the day. No doubt it was just his instincts that were all out of whack because of Harper.

Harper.

He hadn't been able to stop thinking of her. It took everything in him to keep from running back to his cabin and claiming her for his own. But despite the fact that she'd just suffered an injury, even a slight one, it was too soon for that type of behavior. Way too soon. She needed time to process what he'd shown her. Axel knew that. Even if he didn't want to admit it. He wasn't going to jeopardize his future with her just because he was impatient.

No, he'd give her time with her friend. Time to think things over. But then he'd go to her and make her understand. They were fated for each other.

"Axel, stop daydreaming and get over here," Kade yelled, pulling Axel out of his thoughts. When Luke told him about Harper, Kade had been pissed. No, pissed was a massive understatement. Kade was furious. Anything to do with the idea of mating angered him. Especially when one of his siblings was involved. Maybe Axel could have understood his little brother's feelings, but that was before. Before he knew what it was like to have such a strong pull toward someone else. Now, everything was different.

"I'm here." Axel made his way to where his brother was hauling supplies into the kitchen. "What's all this for anyway?"

"Do you think a kitchen just runs itself?" Kade snapped. "How do you think all that fresh bread gets made? Magic? No. I've been working my ass off, mixing and kneading and pretending to be a bloody baker, slaving over a hot oven while you've been out there hooking up with females, running through the woods, and God knows what else."

Axel stood, his arms crossed over his chest, and waited Kade out. Finally, he asked, "You done?"

Kade grunted.

"Good." Axel bent to heave a bag of flour up over his shoulder. "Feel better?"

"I'd feel better if you'd send her home."

"Not going to happen."

Kade picked up a bag of sugar and pushed past Axel as they headed into the kitchen. "Does she even want to stay? I mean, does she know the truth?"

"She knows." Axel avoided the first part of the question. He couldn't bear to think of any answer that wasn't yes. Harper had to stay with him. He already knew from the bottom of his soul that he'd be shattered if she chose to leave.

"Mates are nothing but trouble."

"Don't knock it till you've tried it. You never know, Kade. A mate might be just what you need." He tossed the bag of flour on the counter and turned to grab another one, but Kade stopped him with a shove to the shoulder. "What the—"

"Are you serious?" Kade glared at him. Rage came off his little brother in waves that shocked Axel. "A mate is what tore this family apart. Twice. Remember?"

"It's not like I could forget."

"First Mom and then Kira. They destroyed everything by choosing a mate. Is that what you're going to do, too? Ruin everything we've been working for?"

Axel squared up with him. "I'm not going to ruin a damn thing," he said. "I'm going to make things better."

"For who?"

"For *me.*"

Something Axel didn't recognize flashed in Kade's eyes and he backed down. "I hope it's worth it," he muttered as he shoved past him to get more supplies.

"*She's* worth it," Axel corrected him. He watched Kade walk right past the pile of supplies and go outside. *Good.* He needed some air. Maybe he'd even let himself shift and go for a run. If anyone needed to get in touch with their bear, it was Kade. Too bad he resisted it so much. "Stubborn ass," he muttered under his breath.

"Who's a stubborn ass? Besides you, I mean."

Axel turned to see Luke come through the kitchen door. He'd been making sure their guests were situated and had their choice of activities to participate in.

"I was referring to our little brother." He pointed in the direction Kade had disappeared.

"Ah." Luke nodded and tried not to smile. "He's not very happy with you."

"How do you know?"

"It doesn't take a rocket scientist to figure that one out. You're his big brother—you're supposed to keep everything running smoothly and not rock the boat."

"You think I'm rocking the boat?"

Luke laughed and raised his eyebrow in response.

"I'm not," Axel said. "I can't help what I feel. It's unlike anything I've ever experienced. It's all-consuming. It's—"

"Mating." Luke shook his head. "Look, I don't know how I feel about the whole thing, but I do know that mating isn't something you can pick and choose."

"So you believe in it?" He didn't even try to hide his surprise. Of both his brothers, Axel didn't expect Luke to believe in mates. Let alone fated mates. He knew Kade believed—that's why he got so worked up about it—but Luke?

"Of course I do. But I also believe it's a lot more complicated than you're making it out to be. Especially when that mate doesn't know about her bear."

Luke's words caught him off guard. "What do you mean, know about her bear? You sensed it too?"

HIs brother shook his head. "Seriously? Do you really think you're the only one around here with any instincts at all? Of course I sensed it. Probably before you did since you were so clouded by pheromones and feelings and shit. Harper definitely has some bear in her. But she has no idea. And she probably can't shift or anything, but it would explain why you're so strongly mated to her."

Axel nodded. His little brother never failed to surprise

him, and this was definitely no exception.

"Speaking of Harper…" Axel's body responded instantly to the mention of her name. "She's looking for you. Nina came back to the Den a minute ago and told me she was awake and wanting to talk to you."

Axel didn't stick around to hear anything else. If Harper wanted him, he'd be there.

As Harper sat back into the bed and told Nina all about her time with Axel, leaving out some of the juicier details—especially the ones that included him being a bear—something strange happened. The more she talked, the more a sense of peace came over her. Where she'd been frantic and uneasy not long before, now as she spoke about Axel, everything just felt *right*.

It was ridiculous that she could have feelings for a man so quickly, but that's exactly what was happening. She definitely had feelings. Even Nina had noticed.

"You like him," she teased and nudged Harper in the ribs. "You *really* like him."

"I do." She didn't even try to hide the smile that crossed her face. "I know it's crazy, but—"

"Why is it crazy?"

"Because it's all happening so fast. I'm not supposed to fall in love so quickly and with a…it doesn't make any sense."

"It doesn't have to make sense." Nina flopped on the bed and propped her head up with her hand. "And who says you aren't supposed to fall in love so quickly? Where is that rule written?"

Harper shook her head. She knew what Nina was saying, but still…it was ludicrous to fall for someone so quickly. Especially when there was no way a relationship could work. They were from two different worlds. "Weren't you just saying a minute ago that it was probably just good sex that was clouding my brain?"

Nina shrugged. "That was before I heard you talk about him," she said with a smile on her face. "It's written all over you. You love him. Even I can see that."

"It's just that, logically, this can't work out."

"Logically?" Nina snorted. "Who said there was anything logical about love?"

"I don't know why you keep saying that. It's not like it's *love*."

"Then what is it?"

She couldn't answer that because whatever she said would be a lie. It *was* love. It was definitely love and it didn't matter if it made sense or not.

She loved him.

Instead of answering, Harper buried her face in a pillow and let out a little scream while Nina laughed. When Nina took the pillow away, Harper was laughing as well. "It's all so crazy."

"Yes, it is," her best friend agreed. "And so fantastic. You're way overdue for some crazy."

Harper couldn't disagree with that. But despite all the happy feelings, she was still confused about a few details and she needed to find Axel and talk to him. There were a few things that still bothered her. And one really big, furry, animalistic thing.

"Hey." Harper scooted back on the bed. "Do you think you can do something for me? Can you head down to the Den and tell Axel I want to talk to him? I just want to freshen up before I do."

"How's your foot?"

Dammit. She'd forgotten about her foot. She wiggled it a bit.

"It's actually feeling better. It'll be okay." It was only a small lie. It *was* feeling better. A lot better. She probably shouldn't be walking on it, but she needed to see Axel. It was a need, deep inside her. Just like the feelings of love she was having, she couldn't explain the driving desire to be in his presence either. So many unexplainable feelings.

"I'll just take my time," she said. "I'm sure it will feel better if I get moving on it."

"Okay. If you're sure." Nina jumped up off the bed and straightened her shirt. "I have a few things to check on with the article, too. So as much as I've enjoyed hearing all about your lover boy, I really should get going."

Harper waited until Nina left before she tried to stand on her foot. She gingerly put a little weight on it. *Not too bad.* So she stood and immediately sat back on the bed with a grimace. *Well, it wasn't as bad as before.* But a few more minutes of rest wouldn't hurt.

She lay on the bed and contemplated her options for a moment. Her cell phone rang on the bedside table, making her decision for her. Harper reached for the phone, happy enough to stay propped up in the comfy bed for a few more moments instead of trying to navigate her way on a sore foot.

She glanced at the number on the screen. *John Kendrick.* A wave of unease washed through her. Hopefully he'd have good news for her, but somehow she wasn't so sure.

"Hi, John."

"I'm glad I caught you, Harper. I have some news."

Right to the point. Harper could respect that. Especially in a lawyer she was paying by the hour. "What's up?"

"Are you sitting down?"

Harper glanced around at the bed she hadn't managed to leave yet. "Sure am. Now tell me you've found a hole in Trent's case or something equally damning to shut him down."

"I wish I could. I know there has to be something, but he's obviously been planning this little stunt for some time, because he seems to have thought of every angle and covered all his tracks." Harper shook his head and started to object, but John beat her to it. "But I know his type," John continued. "And they always make mistakes. There will be something; we just need to find it."

"There has to be." Harper racked her brain for a hint of something, anything that she could think of that would incriminate Trent. They may have had a totally loveless marriage, but they'd still lived together. They'd been friends. At least she'd thought they were. Clearly, she'd been wrong. She'd been wrong about a lot of things. But surely she should have noticed something. "Clark." The name popped into her head so suddenly she wasn't even sure she'd spoken aloud.

"Who's Clark?"

"Clark Rosswell. He was one of Trent's…assistants. He was totally loyal to him. In all kinds of ways, if you know what I mean?" She shook her head just remembering how the young man had thrown himself at her husband. Never mind that even thinking the word *husband* made her cringe. In retrospect, Harper couldn't believe how she'd let so many years go by living the status quo. In only a few days, Axel had taught her that she deserved better. Oh, she deserved so much better. She'd never go back to that life again. "Anyway," she refocused her thoughts, "I don't know it for sure, but I'm pretty sure they had an affair."

"You mean, he cheated on you?"

"No." She had to bite her lip to keep from laughing out loud. "I mean, yes. But that was the norm. What I meant was, he cheated on Blake with this kid and I don't know all the details or anything." She shuddered at the thought.

"But I'm pretty sure when Blake found out, he wasn't very happy. Clark was 'let go' shortly after that, and he put up a fuss about it, too. I'm willing to bet he knows something about what was going on and if my suspicions are correct, he might be willing to talk about it."

John chuckled and Harper could just imagine him shaking his head on the other end of the line. She'd never met the man, but she knew she'd like him when she finally did and she couldn't wait to thank him in person for all his work on her behalf. "I can't believe you put up with so much, for so long, Harper. This all sounds like a soap opera."

She sighed and leaned her head back against the headboard. "Don't I know it."

"Well, not to worry, okay? I have a private investigator who I use, and if anyone can get the dirt we need to shut these guys down, it'll be him. I just need you to lay low for a while, okay? Does anyone know where you are?"

Harper shook her head. "No," she said, but quickly amended, "I mean, I'm with Nina and she's writing an article about Grizzly Ridge, but there's no reason anyone would think I'm with her." She felt a twinge of uncertainty. *Would anyone suspect she was with Nina?* Trent might... *No.* She couldn't worry about that.

"Good," John was saying. "We don't want to give Trent any ammunition to use against you. Either real or construed. And from what I've seen, your ex is an expert at twisting information to suit his needs."

"That's what makes him such a good public relations manager." She squeezed her eyes shut. In all of her years putting up with Trent's choices, she never would have thought he'd hurt her so badly. His betrayal stung. Deeply.

CHAPTER TEN

Axel tried twice to get out of the main lodge and back up to his cabin to Harper, but both times his efforts were thwarted by management tasks that needed his immediate attention. He'd considered putting them off, and returning the calls and making the reservations later, after he spoke with Harper. But he couldn't. Not when his brothers were both so clearly threatened by the idea of Harper in his life and what that might mean for Grizzly Ridge. He needed to prove to them that having a mate was only going to make him a better man. Not the other way around.

Taking care of his work hadn't taken long, but it had taken long enough and by the time he'd finished in his office, he was more than a little anxious to get to Harper and make sure she was okay. He tried to sneak out the side door of the Den but the moment he opened the door, he regretted his decision.

"Hey," the man he vaguely remembered as Kevin called to him. They were sitting by the fire pit; the other man stared intently at his camera. "Can I ask you a few questions?"

Axel shook his head reflexively. "You know, I don't really have a minute right now. Maybe you could find my brother Luke? He can answer any of your questions." He tried to keep walking, but then Kevin stood there in his path.

Axel clenched his hands into fists at his side and tried to swallow the growl that threatened to escape. These jokers were keeping him from his mate, and whether Luke thought his instincts were clouded or not, he didn't like them. Not at all.

"Really, it will only take a minute, man. I just want to know about your guests?"

Something in the man's voice set Axel on alert. He stood tall, towering over the smaller man. "Guests?" Alarm bells went off in his head, but he kept his composure. "What makes you think we have any yet?"

"Just a hunch," Bruce said. "And the truckload of businessmen who showed up when we did. Are they the only guests you have? Or are there others?"

Kevin elbowed his buddy and regained control over the situation. "Anyway, we'd like to talk to them," Kevin said. "Some of them anyway." If he'd noticed Axel's animosity, he didn't show it. "It would be good for the piece to see what kind of guests the Ridge is attracting and what they think of their experience here. More of a real-life perspective, ya know?"

He didn't. "I don't think so."

"It would be good to get their photographs, too."

Axel turned slowly toward the photographer who'd continued to chime into the conversation. He shot him a glare and the man looked back down at his camera.

"Definitely not." Axel wanted to grab both men by the back of their necks and drag them off the mountain and far away from his mate, but on some level he was cognizant that he still had a business to run and he couldn't risk them writing anything negative about Grizzly Ridge.

But he also couldn't risk them around his mate. Not yet. Not until he figured out whether they could be trusted or not.

Damn. Was that what it was going to be like from now on? Now that he'd found her, was he going to be suspicious of everyone she came into contact with? Not because he didn't trust her, but because he was protecting her?

He shook off the thought. Surely this would pass. It was just a phase. Especially because it was all new. So new he hadn't even had a chance to check in with Harper to make sure she felt the same way. First things first, though. "Look." He refocused on the man in front of him. "I'm not trying to be difficult, but our guests' privacy is of the utmost importance to us. We have a few new arrivals, as you saw. We had a group from New York who came in. Maybe they'd be willing to be interviewed. In the meantime, I'll go find Luke for you, and he'll be sure to run you through all the activities Grizzly Ridge has to offer."

Kevin opened his mouth, likely to object, but Axel was already walking away. "Wait right here—I'll go get him."

He tried to swallow his impatience when all he really wanted to do was get to Harper. Fortunately, he ran into Luke and Nina as soon as he stepped back into the Den.

"I thought you were going to find Harper?"

"I was," he answered her. "I am. But those damn reporters got in my way." He turned to Luke and started to explain what he needed from him, but Nina interrupted.

"Reporters? What reporters?"

"The new arrivals who showed up unexpectedly," Luke explained. "We didn't know they were coming, but we can't afford to turn away any press."

"Press?" Nina looked confused. "I'm *press*. I wrote a piece for *Lifestyle*. I can't imagine better press than that. *And* I posted a teaser online already. Why do you need more coverage?"

"You put something online already?" Axel's mind spun. "You didn't mention Harper, did you?"

"Of course not. I always mention a traveling companion, but that's it." Nina waved his concern away. "Who are these guys, anyway?"

"Kevin something and Bruce something," Luke said. "I don't remember. I don't suppose you know them?"

"Well, based on that information..." She rolled her eyes. "No." Nina laughed. "But maybe I'd recognize them if I saw them. Let's go find them."

"That's a good idea," Axel said. "There's something I don't like about these guys."

"You don't like anyone right now," Luke said pointedly as he shot Axel a look. "Not since you and—"

"Don't say another word." Axel pulled his shoulders back and stepped up to Luke. He didn't want to, but if his brother was going to provoke him, he'd do what was needed to remind Luke who the alpha was. And his little brother clearly had something he needed to say. Something Axel didn't want to hear.

Luke stood his ground for a moment, but finally shook his head and looked away. "You know what," he said. "I won't say anything. Not yet, anyway. But if you don't pull it together soon, *big brother*, then we *are* going to have a conversation."

Nina looked between the two brothers, concern on her face. He didn't want to scare Nina. Not only because she was a guest, but because she was Harper's best friend and he was pretty sure he'd already done enough scaring of her earlier. Which he needed to go fix. Now.

"So...are we going to go find this Bruce and Kevin or what? Because I can also do a little digging into it and see who they work for, what kind of reputation they have…that kind of thing."

"Yes," Axel answered quickly. "That's a good idea. The more information we have about them, the better. I'd like to think they're legitimate." He made a point to look at Luke when he said that. "But we need to be careful. In the meantime, Luke, I need you to set them up with enough activities to keep them busy until they can get their asses back down to Blackwood Ranch," he ordered his brother, more to make his point about who was in charge than anything else.

Luke bristled, but nodded.

"Good." Axel turned to make his exit. "I have some business to take care of."

"Sure you do."

His hands clenched into fists and he growled as he turned to face his brother again. "Watch it, Luke."

"I mean it." Luke spoke through gritted teeth. "Sort it out, Axel. Quickly."

Axel heard what his brother didn't say. Grizzly Ridge and all of their futures depended on Axel's focus. Focus that was completely consumed by his mate. Luke might be reining himself in for the time being, but he could only tolerate so much before he hit his limit. And he was almost there.

A sharp rap followed by the door to the cabin flying open and banging against the wall jolted Harper awake. Instantly, she was on edge but when she saw Axel in the door, looking rugged, and wild, and so damn sexy, she relaxed a little. But just a little. She still had a lot of unanswered questions.

A lot.

She pulled her legs up to her chest and wrapped her arms around them, hugging herself.

"I didn't mean to wake you." He stepped into the room. "I didn't realize you were sleeping."

"I must have dozed off." She smiled a little. "I was talking to John and it was all so…never mind. I guess I just needed a little rest. It's been kind of a crazy day."

Axel's handsome face was instantly lined with concern. He sat on the edge of the bed. Far enough away to give her space, but close enough that she felt calmed by his presence. Despite everything that happened in the woods—things she still couldn't begin to wrap her head around—just being close to him calmed her in a way that felt almost instinctual.

"Harper, about what happened earlier. I need you to understand…" He looked down at the quilt for a moment, but she waited and when he looked up again, he looked her directly in the eyes. "I love you, Harper."

She felt as if she'd been slapped backward. *Love?* After only a few days? It was ridiculous. And…as the shock of the words faded, a different feeling replaced it. But she couldn't quite put her finger on it. She opened her mouth, but closed it again.

"Don't say anything."

She couldn't even if she wanted to.

"I need you to just listen for a minute, okay?"

She nodded.

"I'll explain everything."

"Everything?"

He nodded and scooted closer to her on the bed. The mattress shifted under his weight and Harper's leg pressed up against the hard length of his thigh. The heat of him burned through the layers of their clothes and warmed her. "I know this sounds crazy," he began. "But I'm not an ordinary man."

Well, she knew that. From the moment she'd laid eyes on him, she'd known there was not one little thing that was *normal* about Axel Jackson.

"The bear you saw in the woods," he continued, his eyes holding hers with their deep gaze. "That was me." She shook her head as a reflex, although deep down she already know he spoke the truth. "I know it sounds crazy, but I'm a shifter. It's not like in the movies or anything. I'm not evil or dangerous or anything." He spoke quickly, obviously nervous about what he was telling her. His nervousness endeared him to her a little more and she reached for his hand. The relief in his face at her small gesture was clear and when he continued speaking, he calmed down. "The bear inside of me is an important part of who I am. It's as much a part of me as…well, anything. I know all of this sounds crazy, but—"

"It doesn't." She couldn't explain it, but it didn't sound crazy at all. In fact, it all made perfect sense to her. *Axel was a bear.* Just thinking those words and not wanting to run screaming for the hills was insane. But at the same time, it wasn't.

"Do you have any questions about it? Anything you want to know?"

She laughed and pulled herself down the bed to be closer to him. "Questions? Oh, I have questions. Lots of them, but…" One question did pop into her head above all others. "You said you loved me." He nodded. "How? I mean, *love*…so quickly…it doesn't make sense."

"It does make sense." He smiled and cupped her face in his large hands. "You're my mate. We're meant to be together."

She would have shaken her head if he hadn't been holding her firmly in his gentle grip. "That doesn't make sense."

"Everything I just told you, and *that* doesn't make sense?" His thumbs stroked gentle circles on her cheek, calming her with their movement. "I never believed in it myself, but my little sister sure did." His eyes took on a faraway look for a moment before refocusing on her. "In the bear world, there's a legend about fated mates and how there's only one bear out there for each of us. The perfect match. And when we meet him or her, we'll know it instinctively."

Instinctively. The word resonated.

"Wait?" Another word resonated. "What did you say?"

"Instinct?"

"No." She shook her head, releasing herself from his hands. "About a bear. There only being one *bear* for each of you. How can it be that you think I'm your mate?"

"I *know* you're my mate."

"But I'm not a bear."

Axel didn't say anything right away, but just looked at her. His intense eyes fixed on her with a gaze so full of love and need and...knowledge.

"Axel?" Harper's mind spun with everything he hadn't said. A *bear?* That didn't make any sense. Axel being a bear...okay. But *her?* No. That wasn't possible. Not that any of it was possible, not really, but... "I can't be," she said, finally. "I'd know. I would have known."

"I wasn't sure at first either, but..." He nodded and his hand squeezed her thigh, stilling her. "Did you feel an instant attraction to me?"

She nodded.

"When we made love, did it feel...*different?*"

"Well, yes. But that's only because I've never had..." She was going to say that she'd never felt the way she felt about Axel with anyone else. But wasn't that the point of what he was saying? "When I'm with you…" she started. The thoughts formulated in her head. "I feel at peace. Like I'm where I'm supposed to be. With you, I feel like I'm right where I should be."

He couldn't contain the smile that lit up his face. "That's because you're my mate." Before she could say anything else, he continued to explain. "There are more of us than you might think. In fact, many of us don't even know that we have shifter blood in us." He stopped and squeezed her hand.

"So, you think…"

"I think you have some shifter in you, Harper. Maybe not a full-blooded shifter. But somewhere along the line…there is definitely bear blood in you."

Harper shook her head, but even as she did, what Axel was saying made perfect sense. Well, maybe not *perfect* sense. But something told her that she couldn't just dismiss what he was saying out of hand. Something deep inside her knew what he was saying was true. "I never knew my father," she said. "When I was old enough, my mom told me she'd met him on a trip to Canada with her girlfriends. She fell hard for him, but after she returned home and found out she was pregnant, she couldn't get in touch with him again. Do you think…"

Axel nodded and Harper laughed. "That's ridiculous," she said.

"Is it?"

He reached for her and pulled her easily into his arms. With him, she felt so tiny, so protected, and so completely…*animal.* The word popped into her head, but it fit the situation perfectly.

Axel leaned closer to her, bringing his lips to her forehead, then the tip of her nose and finally, her lips. He kissed her softly but thoroughly. "Is it really so ridiculous the way we're connected?"

Without a doubt in her mind, Harper shook her head. "No. It's not ridiculous at all." It was her turn to kiss him, and when she did, her whole body lit up with the reaction he never failed to elicit in her. She had to pull away, only to finish saying what she needed to say before her brain was completely clouded with passion for the man. "I have never in my whole life felt about someone the way I feel about you. It might be crazy. It might be too soon. It might be a lot of things. But one thing I know for sure—bear or not, I am absolutely, completely, body and soul, in love with you, Axel Jackson."

It was all he needed to hear. His mate loved him. She was his. He was hers. They would be mated as soon as they consummated that love.

His mouth covered hers and he kissed her long and hard until she made that little whimpering noise that drove him crazy. He wrapped his hand in her hair and tugged her hair to the side so he could kiss his way down her neck. The cotton collar on her t-shirt quickly got in his way and with a swipe, he tore it from her body.

Harper gasped and pulled back. "That's how you...before...you..." She laughed and shook her head. "You're going to need to simmer down with that or I'll need a whole new wardrobe."

"Baby, I'll buy you whatever you need." A surge of love and protectiveness welled up inside him. "I'll give you everything you need from now until the end of time. I love you. You're my mate and I swear you'll never want for anything."

Harper laughed a little and ducked her head. "Those

sound oddly like wedding vows, Axel."

"No." He shook his head. "Not wedding vows. Much more meaningful than that. We're mates and we'll be connected forever as soon as we finish mating. I'm just making sure you—"

"Wait." She put a hand on his chest but didn't push him away. "We've already had sex. Does that mean we're mated?"

He should have explained it to her. It was too easy to take for granted that she already knew everything about the bear world. He was going to have to keep reminding himself that she was new to all of this. He'd have to be patient. With Harper, that was never going to be a problem. He had all the time in the world for her. "No," Axel said slowly. "The mating process is really quite simple and I don't want you to be scared." He could see on her face that was the wrong choice of words. "It won't hurt. Not really. Well, to be honest…I don't really know."

"You don't know?"

"Well, I haven't done it before. You're my mate."

She laughed a little. It helped defuse the tension. "True, I guess. So tell me…"

"I'm going to bite you." Again, it was the wrong thing to say. But it was the truth. He reached for her, trailing his fingers slowly down her neck until she closed her eyes from the pleasure of the touch. It never failed to affect him, the way she responded so readily to him. "It'll be fine." He pressed his lips to the sensitive skin below her ear and felt her shudder in need. "I promise."

Axel moved slowly, pressing Harper back into the pillows until he was on top of her, surrounding her. She looked so beautiful laying beneath him, with her hair spread over the pillow, her luscious full breasts bared to him, and her face flushed with need for him. He moved so he could take one perfect breast in his mouth. Her nipple hardened to a firm peak almost instantly and he flicked his tongue back and forth until she moaned from the pleasure of it. His hands kneaded the soft flesh while his thumb brushed over the other nipple, giving it the attention he knew it also craved.

"God, you have the most beautiful tits." He buried his face between them, allowing himself a moment to enjoy the perfection of his curvy mate before he kissed his way down her body until he reached her belt. Axel's first instinct was to rip her jeans from her body, but he stopped himself and fumbled with her belt instead.

"Get rid of it." Harper's eyes were heavy with desire as she ordered him to destroy her clothes. She needed him as bad as he needed her.

Axel growled and did as she wished. *His mate, perfect in every way.*

When she was stripped bare to him, Axel resumed his worship of her body, kissing, licking, and nibbling until he reached her apex. He slicked a finger through her heat. She was so wet. So ready for him. The knowledge that he could turn her on so quickly, so easily, only fueled his desire. He added another finger and pressed inside her, making her gasp. He grinned and moved in and out of her while his thumb brushed over her sensitive nub just enough to build her to a frenzy of need. He instinctively knew what she needed, what she craved from him. He was more than happy to give it to her. He'd give her everything she wanted.

Always.

"Axel?"

He paused his movements and looked up in question at her gorgeous face, made even more stunning by the flush of passion on her cheeks.

"Axel, I need you. Now."

Before he could respond, her hands reached up and tugged on his shirt. He could have sworn he heard a small growl come from his mate. It was a sound that made his already hard dick twitch against his zipper. Helping her, he yanked his shirt over his head and shucked his jeans down, freeing himself for her.

Once again, he straddled her, poised at her entrance. He waited until her eyes met his. The love he felt for her matched the look in her eyes and he knew without a doubt that this would be a life-changing moment for both of them. He bent to kiss her lips, deeply and possessively as he slid into her heat.

Harper gasped into his open mouth and he swallowed her groan as her body grew accustomed to his size. He had to pause, just for a moment. Just long enough to slow his heartbeat. She felt so damn good. Better than anyone or anything else he'd ever experienced. Because he'd never been in love before. He'd never had his mate before. But now that he'd found her…there'd never be anything or anyone who could ever compare.

When Axel entered her, it was different than anything she'd ever felt before. Even different than their first time. All Harper's senses were heightened this time. Every part of her body was alive with sensation. It took a moment to grow used to his size because he felt so damn good she thought she might explode from the inside if he moved.

But then he did move, and it was amazing. With every stroke and thrust, the need built in her. He pulled back, until only the tip of him was in her, before driving back inside, deeper than before. She wrapped her legs around him, pulling him tighter to her.

"Axel, I…" Words failed her as he drove into her, her body accepting everything he could give. Instead of words, she pulled his head down to hers and kissed him hard to communicate in the only way she could.

A pressure deep down began to build and Harper threw her head back, gasping for air as the feeling inside her grew stronger. She'd had orgasms before, but the storm brewing inside her was different. She squirmed under him, trying to move away, but not sure why considering the feelings he was giving her were unlike anything she'd ever experienced. Needing a release, Harper dug her nails into Axel's muscled back.

"That's right, baby. Let it happen."

She wanted to ask him what was happening, what she needed to let happen, but there was no way Harper could formulate a thought.

"It's your bear," Axel whispered in a hot breath into her ear as if he'd just read her mind. "Don't fight it—just let her out."

Harper had no idea what *letting her out* would mean, but she stopped her mind from asking questions she didn't have answers to and focused on the sensations that ripped through her body. She thrust her hips up against Axel's, needing him deeper, stronger. Needing something she couldn't even put into words. Her nails raked across his back and he groaned with the pleasure of it, but the sound of it barely registered—Harper was so consumed by keeping up with everything her body was throwing at her.

Finally, she could feel her body reach the point of no return; she was going to orgasm like never before. Harper threw her head back and a noise she didn't recognize as her own escaped her as the pressure built to the point of explosion.

"You are so fucking sexy." Axel dropped his mouth to her neck and kissed her hard as he thrust into her one final time, taking his own pleasure as her orgasm shattered through her. She could see nothing, hear nothing, and feel nothing but the weight of Axel on top of her and inside her as she came completely apart under him with a force she never could have expected.

When she finally opened her eyes, he was watching her intently. He stroked her hair back from her forehead, but made no move to leave her body, which Harper was thankful for. She was certain if he withdrew now, she'd feel an emptiness she never had before. She needed him right where he was. At least for another moment longer.

"God, I love you," Axel said, but she didn't see his lips move. He must have seen the confusion in her eyes, because he smiled a little and explained, "I didn't know if it would be possible, but I've heard stories of mates who could communicate without speech. Mostly when they're in their bear form, but legend has it that fated mates can communicate when they're…well…*joined*."

Harper giggled at his choice of words. "So we can— wait! Mates? You mean, we're…"

"Mated."

The word hung in the air. "But I…you didn't…"

"Bite you?"

She nodded.

"Babe, I did."

Her mind swirled. He didn't; she would have known. She would have felt it. Or would she have? There'd been a lot of intense feelings going on. A lot of sensation. He kissed her gently on the lips and pushed himself off her body. She immediately felt his absence.

"Give me a second." Axel disappeared into the bathroom and returned a moment later with a warm washcloth and a handheld mirror. "Look."

When she took the mirror from him, all she could see was a very tousled, very well sexed version of herself staring back at her, but slowly she moved the mirror down and almost dropped it when she saw the evidence of their mating: a bite mark at the base of her neck, directly over her collarbone. The teeth marks were clearly defined and they were most definitely *not* human. Her free hand crept up and tentatively touched the wound, because that's what it was. A wound.

"But...how did you...I don't..."

Axel's hand slid up to cover hers, and the bite mark. "You were a little distracted." His grin said everything else and Harper couldn't help but laugh.

"I was *very* distracted."

"Does it hurt?" He removed her hand and used a finger to gently trace her neck. "Now that you know it's there?"

Harper shook her head. "No. It doesn't. Well, it's a little sore maybe. But I like it." She twisted her neck back and forth, testing it. "It's like a reminder of you and...us."

"I like it that you're marked. Now everyone will know I'm yours."

"I'm yours." She tested the words on her tongue. They sounded just right.

"You're mine." He kissed her thoroughly. "And I'm yours. Always." When their lips met again, the kiss held a different kind of passion. They were connected now more than ever, and she could happily lose herself in him forever.

A moment later, a crash at the window jolted them apart, and not even a second after that, Axel was up out of bed and out the door. Harper grabbed the bed sheet and wrapped it around her body; forgetting momentarily about her foot, she jumped out of bed to follow him. She vaguely acknowledged that her foot felt a bit stiff, but hardly hurt anymore. She made her way to the window to see what was happening.

As much as Harper strained her neck, she couldn't see anything. She heard Axel yelling, calling out to whomever or whatever had been at their window. A moment later, the door opened and her protector—her very naked protector—walked in and shut the door behind him.

"What was it?"

He shook his head. "I couldn't see anything."

"It might have been an animal or a bird."

"Maybe." He didn't look convinced. "I should have gone after it but whatever it was, it was too fast and I could have shifted, but…"

"But what?"

"There are rules." While he spoke, he walked through the room and gathered his clothes. "You can't shift where humans could see you. It's a responsibility to protect people from the truth because mostly it's ourselves we're protecting."

"You shifted in front of me."

Axel tugged his t-shirt over his head and shrugged. "That's different. You're my mate and besides, you *are* a shifter."

"I didn't know it. Besides, I don't know if I can even shift."

"I think you'd surprise yourself. You're sure as hell surprising me." He kissed her quickly and bent to tug his jeans on. "Get dressed."

"Where are we going?" She wanted to talk about shifting some more. She hadn't even considered it as an option until just right then, and now that the idea was in her head she wanted to talk about it some more. She wanted to explore the idea.

"I'm taking you to the Den," he said. "You'll be safe

there."

"I'm not safe here?" A shock of fear shot through her, but was gone just as quickly, knowing Axel was there.

"Not until I figure out what or who was out there. I want you where you can be protected. Just in case."

Harper nodded and accepted the clothes Axel had pulled out of the drawer and handed her. She'd always been a woman who could look after herself—hell, she still was—but it was pretty damn nice to have someone who cared enough to look after her, too. She couldn't deny that.

CHAPTER ELEVEN

The last thing Axel wanted to do was leave Harper alone. But she'd be safe at the Den. He'd carried her through the woods and set her up on the couch in front of the fireplace with a cup of coffee and a book. She said her foot hardly hurt, and it would be totally healed soon. Shifters healed quickly, and if she'd been a full-blooded bear, she would already be good as new; it was just taking her a little longer. Not that he minded carrying her and having her heat pressed up against his body—that was something he could definitely get used to. He'd carry her everywhere, but he was pretty sure that would be taking the protective thing a little too far. As it was, she'd protested about being left behind, just the way he knew his mate would. She was a strong woman who liked to be in control, but she was going to have to get used to him taking the lead some of the time and taking care of her, because there was nothing in the world he wanted to do more.

And that's why he needed to leave her for a few minutes. He needed to figure out what had been outside of the cabin. It might have been a raccoon or a bird. But he didn't think so. His instincts were clouded at the moment, that was for sure, but since he'd mated with Harper and finally claimed her for his own, they'd cleared somewhat.

But not enough.

He needed his brothers.

Kade was in the kitchen. "I need your help."

"Hello to you, too, big brother." Kade slammed a pot onto the countertop.

"Hello," Axel amended. "I need your help."

"Of course you do. That's all anyone ever needs from me around here."

Perfect. Kade was in a mood. His little brother had always been the moody one in the family, but it was a problem that had been growing increasingly worse ever since he'd been denying his bear. He was getting downright impossible to deal with some days.

"Right." Axel chose to ignore Kade's drama. "It's about my mate."

"Of course it is."

Axel slammed his fist down on the counter, rattling the jars of spices Kade had collected. "Are you done?" His brother glared at him in response. "Because this is serious."

"It would have to be, if it's for your *mate*."

Axel's fists flexed next to him and he twitched to punch his brother. Kade obviously needed a reminder about who exactly was in charge. "I'll give you one more chance, Kade. But that's it. I'm not in the mood today. And I don't have time to deal with this."

Kade looked as if he was going to challenge Axel again, but he swallowed hard and crossed his thick arms over his chest. "What do you need?"

It was as close as he was going to get to acceptance, so Axel explained the situation and gave him two choices. "You can stay here and protect my mate, or you can come with me and hunt whatever it was that was outside my window."

They both knew that it wasn't a choice. Not for Kade. Going with Axel to hunt the threat would mean shifting. And Kade flat out refused to do that. Having him at the Den to protect Harper, even when he was surly, didn't worry Axel in the least, because even if Kade struggled with the very idea of a mate, he was a fierce protector and more than that, he was loyal. Harper would be safe with Kade. Of that, he had no doubt.

"I'll be here," Kade said. "If anything or anyone threatens her, I'll take care of it."

As an afterthought, Axel turned and asked, "Where are the guests?" The last thing he needed was a threat running around when they had their first paying guests at the Ridge.

Kade shook his head. "Don't worry. They're with Nina, down at Blackwood. Brian called to reschedule their trail ride for this afternoon. I didn't think it would be a problem."

"It's perfect," he said, "And those reporters?"

Kade shrugged. "No idea, but they didn't go with everyone else."

Axel nodded. It wasn't ideal, but at least there weren't many people around to worry about. He waved absently and left his little brother in the kitchen where he'd found him. Come to think of it, he always found Kade in the kitchen. He worked too hard; maybe they should think about getting him a little help when things settled down. Maybe it would help calm him a little if he had somebody to work with instead of being alone every day. Maybe, but he doubted it. He couldn't think of it at the moment anyway. Axel had bigger problems, and he needed to find Luke to take care of them as soon as possible.

Harper fumed. She wasn't happy about being left in the Den by herself like some weak woman who needed to be coddled. She was perfectly capable of taking care of herself, and even if Axel wanted to be her hero, there was no reason she couldn't be involved in the search.

She wiggled her ankle and flexed her toes. They weren't sore anymore. Tentatively, she tried to stand, aware of the pain that was probably going to drop her back to her ass. But instead of pain radiating through her leg the way it had before, she was able to stand with only a dull throb. Encouraged, she took a step forward. It didn't hurt. At all.

"There's no way." Harper laughed at herself and took a few more steps around the living room. "It's better."

"Of course it's better."

Harper jumped back, startled by the voice.

Had the person who'd been outside the cabin found her? Was she going to be attacked? Axel was wrong; she wouldn't be safe at the Den. A million thoughts flew through her head, but as soon as she turned around and saw Kade with a tray full of cookies, she laughed.

"Am I funny?" He tried to look stern, but Harper could see the smile teasing at the edge of his mouth. Kade wasn't nearly as tough as he liked people to think he was.

"No," she said. "I'm laughing at myself and my crazy imagination. Axel got me all worked up is all."

Kade put the tray down on the table in front of the couch and crossed his arms over his chest. He was really a beast of a man. Axel was a big man, but his little brother was huge. "I see that's not all he did." Kade nodded toward Harper.

Her hand flew to her neck where the scarf she'd wrapped had slipped. She hastily tugged it back into position but it was too late.

"You're mated." It was a statement, not a question.

"We are."

Kade grunted something she couldn't make out and shook his head.

"What was that?" Axel had told her that Kade didn't believe in mating, that his opinion was only a negative one—nothing good could come from mating. She'd only been mated a few hours, but already she knew in her heart that nothing but positive things could come from it.

"It's nothing," Kade said. "I baked some cookies."

"You baked me cookies?"

"I just baked them. You happen to be here."

Harper smiled to herself. Deep down, Kade definitely had a soft spot. *Maybe all he needed was a mate of his own?* "Hey, where's Nina?" Her friend popped into her head, not that she'd be a good mate for Kade, but it was always an option... *No.* Knowing Nina, it was definitely not an option.

"She went with the others down to Blackwood Ranch for a trail ride."

"Oh." Harper was disappointed. She would have loved to share with her friend about what had happened between her and Axel. Not that she really knew how to explain things, but still, it would be nice to be able to talk to her girlfriend about things. But there was probably some cute businessman to flirt with or something. It occurred to Harper that she hadn't even seen the new guests yet. She'd been so occupied with her own drama she hadn't noticed that life kept moving without her.

"Did you need something? Whatever you need, I can...get it for you." He shifted from foot to foot, obviously uncomfortable and itching to get away.

Harper laughed. "I'm good. Now I have cookies." She picked one up and took a bite. The buttery flavor exploded on her tongue. "Delicious cookies," she said through a mouthful. "I'm just going to curl up with this book and eat cookies until Axel comes back."

Kade looked unsure.

"Honestly," she said. "I'm fine. Go do whatever you need to do. I'm not going anywhere."

"Oh, I know you're not going anywhere. You're on my watch. But I do need to put the bread in the oven if we're going to have it for dinner."

"Go." Harper waved him away. "Honestly, I'm fine."

Kade hesitated for a moment and finally nodded. "Okay. Call me if you need anything. I'll just be in there."

Harper laughed. "Go. It's not like I'll need anything."

And she didn't either. The book she'd brought with her turned out to actually be pretty good. It had been so long since she'd allowed herself the time to read for fun and for the life of her, she couldn't remember why. Before she knew it, she was so immersed in the love story, she'd eaten half the plate of cookies and didn't even notice when someone came down the stairs and joined her on the couch. It wasn't until the cushion sank with the weight of him that Harper jostled, shocked by the intrusion in her reading.

"Hello, Harper," the man said.

A flash of fear that quickly turned to disgust moved through her.

"Trent."

"It's Kevin around here." Trent laughed, a sound that made Harper's stomach turn.

"What are you doing here?" It didn't occur to Harper to be scared. After all, she was in the Den; Kade was only a few feet away in the kitchen. He'd be there in an instant if she needed anything. Besides, it was Trent they were talking about.

"I came to see you."

"How did you know I was here?"

His smile, the one she once thought was handsome and welcoming, made her want to stab him with something sharp, or better yet, blunt and rusty. "If you're trying to hide," he said, his voice filled with cocky self-assurance, "you should tell your friend to be a little more careful about what she publishes. It doesn't take a genius to figure out that you were her traveling companion to an out-of-the-way Montana retreat."

Harper shook her head. She should have known better about what Nina was writing. But there was no time to worry about it. She refused to focus on details she couldn't change at the moment.

"Who's Kevin?" She shook her head, trying to make sense of his presence and what he'd said.

Trent laughed again, the sound worse than before. He waved away her question. "It doesn't matter."

She was pretty sure it did matter. A great deal. But she kept her mouth shut and waited to hear what he had to say.

"I understand you're having a bit of legal trouble," Trent said. "I'm sorry to hear that."

Harper stuffed her hand underneath her to keep from hitting him. "I'm sure you are."

The man she'd once shared a life with leaned in and Harper had to bite the inside of her cheek to keep from shuddering.

"It's only going to get worse," he said. "That is, if you don't cooperate with me."

She should yell for Kade. She should get up and walk into the kitchen herself. But something told her she needed to stick around and hear what he had to say. It couldn't hurt at this point. "What are you talking about?"

Trent pulled out a piece of paper; it looked like a contract of some sort. "Sign this."

Harper shook her head. "No way am I signing something without reading it. Do I look stupid?"

His laugh was gross and Harper could taste bile in her mouth. "No. But you do look like a woman who is going down for embezzlement. And if you don't sign this paper relinquishing me from any wrongdoing, things will get a lot worse for you."

Of course. It wasn't surprising that he'd try to pull something like this. Not really. Nothing about Trent surprised her anymore.

When she didn't answer right away, he flapped the paper in her face. "Sign."

She shook her head. "I'm not signing that." She crossed her arms over her chest. "I had nothing to do with anything. You and Blake planned everything. You were behind the embezzlement, not me. And my lawyer is going to prove it."

"No, he's not." The cold tone and smug look on Trent's face caused Harper's breath to hitch in her throat. She held her breath, determined not to let him see the effect he had on her. "He won't be able to prove a thing," Trent continued. "Because I have a new story, complete with photographic evidence."

"What story could that be?" Even as she asked the question, Harper's stomach sank.

"To sum it up for you," he said with another smirk that she itched to smack off his face. "Basically, it was your plan all along to steal money from the agency in order to build an elaborate love nest in the mountains where you could engage in kinky sex with your lover."

Harper's blood ran cold. What was he talking about? *Love nest? Kinky sex?* But there was one phrase in particular that stuck in her head. *Photographic evidence.*

"It was you," she said. "At the window."

He held an iPad in front of her, pushed a button and the screen came to life with a photo of her and Axel in bed together. He flicked the screen. It was the next picture that took her breath away. Her head was thrown back, her face a mask of divine pleasure. She couldn't see Axel's face because he was bent to her neck...biting her. Mating her.

She ripped the iPad away from him and had to work hard to swallow back the rage that built inside her. *How dare Trent invade her privacy in such a way? How dare he capture such an intimate moment? And worse, try to exploit it.*

She could feel something inside her churn, threaten to explode as she flicked through the pictures. "You had no right."

"That one's my favorite." He ignored her to reach over and point at the photo Harper couldn't stop staring at. "Although it's particularly disgusting. Really, Harper. I didn't take you as the type for a little kink."

Rage boiled within her. "You would have no idea what *type* I am," she said through clenched teeth.

Trent shrugged and picked up the paper again. "Oh, and don't bother deleting them," he said. "We have copies on Blake's laptop."

"Blake?" Of course he'd be there, too. The idea that Trent had not only infiltrated her happiness at the Ridge, but also brought his lover with him to assist in ruining her, only added to the insult.

"Of course." Trent wiggled his eyebrows.

How had she ever considered this man a friend? A partner? The idea made her sick. She didn't know him at all. Which was demonstrated by his coldness as he continued to speak.

"And if you don't sign, the whole story, including the pictures, is going to be sent to the *Times*."

She shook her head. The rage within her swelled, and the urge to attack the man in front of her continued to grow stronger. She couldn't explain it. She'd never been an aggressive person. Sure, she got angry from time to time, but this felt almost...animal.

No.

She couldn't think of that right now. She shook her head, a motion Trent took to be directed toward him.

"Don't bother denying it," he said. "This *is* happening. And it will happen all over the front page of the *Times* tomorrow morning if you don't sign this paper. Now."

Harper stared at the paper. At Trent. Back to the paper. Would he really do it?

Yes.

There was no doubt in her mind that he'd do exactly as he threatened. Surely her lawyer could find something to exonerate her. But would it come in time? She couldn't wait. She couldn't risk it. Because it wasn't only her ass on the line. She glanced around the room. Everything was at stake. For her and Axel.

For Grizzly Ridge.

She didn't have a choice. She took the pen from Trent, but her hand shook so badly she dropped it.

He picked it up and thrust it at her again. "Sign."

If she did this, she would most certainly go to jail for something she didn't do. For crimes Trent committed and set her up for. He'd get away scot-free. But if she didn't sign, Axel and his brothers would be dragged into a messy legal battle. The damage to their reputation and that of Grizzly Ridge would be irreparable. They'd lose everything. Because of her. She couldn't let that happen. She *wouldn't* let it happen.

Her hand shook so violently, she needed to use her left hand to support it. "Okay," she whispered. "I'll sign."

Trent grinned with victory, a sight so repulsive that the rage built inside her once again. But when he thrust the paper in front of her, she swallowed the urge to react violently.

Harper squeezed her eyes for a moment and said a silent apology to Axel for what she was about to do. Her heart physically hurt as she felt it breaking, knowing she could never be with the man she loved, the one she'd finally found. She opened her eyes and poised the pen over the line. The tip was about to touch the paper when the front door crashed open and a roar rocked the room.

With a solid paw to the door, it crashed open and Axel reared up on his hind legs, voicing his displeasure with a roar that filled the space. The reaction of the sleazy reporter, Kevin, would have been almost comical if he hadn't been sitting much too close to Axel's mate, threatening her. He may not have been a physical threat, but without a doubt he was one. And no one threatened his mate.

No one.

Axel roared again; the man fell off the couch and scrambled backward across the floor, searching for escape. There would be no escape for the weasel if he could help it.

Axel's bear lumbered forward, advancing on the man who he was fully prepared to tear limb from limb if it meant Harper would be safe. Something had stopped him in his search out in the woods and he'd just *known* on some level that Harper needed him. He'd never run so fast, crashing through the trees and brush in a wild panic to get to her. He was only mildly aware of Luke chasing him, trying to keep up but totally unable to match Axel's frantic pace. Fueled by the need to protect his mate, he couldn't be stopped.

Kevin held his hands up in a vain effort to protect himself and screamed something incoherent but Axel just snorted and bared his teeth; his advance continued.

"No." Harper's voice stopped him in his tracks. Axel turned his large head toward her. She stepped toward him, tentatively at first, but then more confidently. "Don't hurt him," she said.

Axel growled in response. That wasn't an option. He was definitely going to hurt this man.

Harper touched his snout. She stroked his fur and stared into his eyes. "Don't, Axel," she whispered. "Trent's not worth it."

Trent?

He growled in protest and flicked his gaze back to the man who now stared at them incredulously. *The man who was Harper's ex? Of course.* He'd known his instincts were right about the man from the beginning. He was no good.

"I don't have a choice," she said. "I have to sign it."

Sign what? He didn't know what she was talking about. But Axel didn't need to know the details. Whatever it was Trent was trying to get her to sign was obviously upsetting her. And if it was upsetting her, there was no way in hell she was going to sign anything. That was all he needed to know. Over her shoulder, he saw a piece of paper on the couch. With a lunge and a swipe, his claws shredded the paper, and the couch cushion. He landed on all fours and turned back in the man's direction with another growl. He still had unfinished business to take care of.

Trent, apparently smart enough to see the giant grizzly was once again focused on him, resumed his backward retreat and crawled into the swinging kitchen door, which at that moment opened, revealing Kade, covered in flour. "What the—oh shit."

Axel watched his little brother shake his head, swallow his laughter and then reach down to grab Trent by the scruff of the neck and haul him to his feet. "Not a good idea to piss off a bear," he said, barely containing his laughter.

Trent's head swung back and forth between them. "What the hell is going on here?" His voice shook.

"I think I could ask you the same thing." Kade looked at Harper. "Was this reporter threatening you? Dammit, I knew I shouldn't have—"

"He's not a reporter," Harper said. "I don't know what he told you, but it was lies. It's always lies with Trent."

"Trent?"

Harper nodded sharply. "Yes. He's my ex."

Kade gripped Trent tighter by the collar and gave him an extra shake. "Did he hurt you? I'll—"

"It's fine," Harper said. "I'm fine."

She wasn't fine. Axel's growl rumbled low in his throat. That's why he'd come. He'd sensed her distress. He wasn't even sure how, just that he had.

Kade picked up on Axel's building hostility and directed his questioning back to Trent. "What do you want? What were you doing to her?"

"Nothing."

Even captured, the little weasel was being an insolent prick. Axel took two steps toward him and he cowered in response. "Fine." Trent gave in. "I was trying to get her to sign a—"

"A statement admitting that I was responsible for everything he'd done to my company. He was blackmailing me." Harper moved to the couch and picked up the iPad lying there. Axel knew without looking exactly what was on the screen. Trent had been the noise outside the window of his cabin, which meant he'd seen everything.

His rage renewed, he reared up on his hind legs and let out a deafening roar. There was no doubt in Axel's mind that he'd kill the man if Harper wasn't standing there. He'd taken the most intimate act of their lives, and was using it against them. That was inexcusable.

Harper stilled him with a simple look and gestured toward Trent with her head. The man had pissed his pants. *Good.* It was a small victory, but if he couldn't do what he really wanted to the man, Axel would take what he could get.

"He says he has copies," Harper said.

"Is that true?" Kade, still holding Trent by the neck, shook the man like a rag doll. "Where are the copies?"

"They're gone." They all turned to see Luke in the doorway, holding Bruce—whom Axel suspected wasn't Bruce at all—in a very similar manner as his friend. He dragged the photographer, if that's who he really was, into the Den. When he saw Axel, he tried to turn and run, but Luke held him fast. "I found this asshole trying to sneak out the window. Turns out it's not a very soft landing when you land on a laptop." In his spare hand, Luke held up the shattered machine.

"Blake," Harper said, confirming Axel's suspicions. "Of course."

"Blake, is that…the pictures…dammit." Trent looked as if he might cry.

"Those are the only copies of the pictures?" Harper asked him.

Trent nodded and Axel could see by the defeat in his eyes it was the truth.

Axel could feel his bear weakening. It was too much to demand such physical exertion for so long, and now that the adrenaline was wearing off, he'd need to make his exit soon or risk having to come up with an even more complicated explanation. Despite the fact that Harper was walking straight toward the man who'd just been threatening her, he knew she could handle herself. Especially now that she was surrounded by bears and she was finally aware of her own shifter blood.

With one final snarl in Trent's direction that had him cowering in fear once again, Axel turned and lumbered past Luke and out the front door.

CHAPTER TWELVE

"I still can't believe I missed everything." Nina was curled up on a chair across from where Harper sat wrapped in Axel's arms. He hadn't left her side since he returned from shifting. She knew it must have taken a lot out of him to be in his bear for so long, but she also knew she couldn't fully comprehend it. There was still so much she didn't know. So much she needed to learn. And she would, in time.

"You should be glad you missed it all." Harper still wasn't sure how much to tell Nina, but she'd let the guys handle the explanations to all their guests, who had all thought it was very exciting, but not enough to fight their jet leg, and had retreated to their rooms. The brothers had kept their explanation as close to the truth as possible, leaving out the crucial detail that Axel was the bear who'd come into the Den.

"I still can't believe it…" Nina practically jumped from her seat. "A bear? Right here? Like, in this room?"

They all nodded.

"And the *reporters* were actually Trent and Blake?" Nina shook her head. "No wonder they were avoiding me. I would have outed them right away."

"Obviously." Harper smiled and snuggled back into Axel's chest.

"They must have been freaking out! But what great timing to get Trent to back down on his blackmail." Nina sank back into the chair. "Can you imagine what a great story that would make?"

"No."

"I don't think so."

"Forget about it."

All three brothers spoke at once. It was Axel who spoke up again. "What we mean," he said, "is it probably wouldn't be good for business if word got out that there was a bear in the Den. After all, if guests thought the main lodge wasn't safe, I can't imagine we'd get many bookings. As it is, we offered the New Yorkers a free night because of it."

"True." Nina nodded thoughtfully. "Still. I can't believe I missed it."

Harper smiled kindly. She hated lying to her friend, but it was easier than trying to explain the truth. At least for the time being. And she'd been honest about everything else. Including how she'd handled Trent all on her own.

After Axel had made his exit, she'd felt stronger than ever, buoyed up by some newfound strength and possibly the support of the Jackson brothers around her. Either way, she'd confronted Trent and told him in no uncertain terms that if he didn't take his *lover* and his false story all the way back down the mountain, she was personally going to make their life a living hell.

A point that was backed up by an impeccably timed phone call from her lawyer. John told her his private investigator had found the young man, Clark Rosswell, that Harper had told him about, and he was more than happy to talk about everything he knew. Which, judging from Trent's face when Harper relayed the message, was quite a bit. As they spoke, Clark was making a statement to the police about everything he knew regarding Trent and Blake's plans to embezzle from their company. *Never underestimate the anger of a spurned lover.*

The Jackson brothers had released Trent and Blake into the custody of the local sheriff, an old friend of theirs who promised to return them to the proper authorities in California, after a night or two in local lockup, of course. And the whole mess was cleaned up and back to normal by the time Nina and the New Yorkers returned from their trail ride. Harper still couldn't believe it was all over.

"Still," Nina said. "I'm sorry I missed it all. It would have been something to see."

Harper twisted her head to smile at Axel. "It certainly was," she said before he kissed her.

"You two are so damn cute." Nina smiled. "It's about time you had someone who so clearly worships you."

"I'd do anything for her." Axel stared directly into her eyes when he said it. "Anything," he repeated.

"Speaking of *anything*," Luke said. "How did you get here so fast? We were out in the woods," he said to Nina in explanation. "And all of a sudden, he turned and started running back toward the Den." He left out the part about the fact that Axel was running as a bear. "I mean, you've always been fast," Luke continued. "But you're not *that* fast. I've always been able to beat you before."

"I never had a mate to protect before."

"A *mate*?" Nina looked at them strangely.

"I mean, a *girlfriend*." He emphasized the word and Harper laughed.

Sitting there, snuggled in with the man she loved and her friends, new and old, Harper had never felt such happiness.

"So, now that you're going to be cleared," Nina said, "I suppose you can go home and get back to work."

Axel tensed behind her and pulled Harper closer to him, but he had nothing to worry about. Harper laughed a little. "I'm not going anywhere," she said. "Because I'm already home."

Just low enough so only she could hear, Axel growled in appreciation and nuzzled her neck, tracing his tongue along the spot that marked her as his.

Yes, she was definitely home.

EPILOGUE

It had only been two weeks since Harper had decided to stay with him on Grizzly Ridge, but it felt like a lifetime. A lifetime of joy because Axel had never been so happy or felt so complete as he had now that Harper was by his side. She'd fit right into life at the Ridge, as though she'd always been meant to be there. With her knowledge in public relations, Harper had already proved to be invaluable with marketing efforts, and combined with Nina's article, Grizzly Ridge was booked solid for the next six months. Business was booming, and their relationship was thriving. Even his brothers had admitted that having Harper around was a good thing.

Now if he could only convince them that maybe they should look for mates of their own, they could all be as happy as Axel was. But he couldn't focus on that now. His focus was entirely on his own mate and the night he'd promised her.

She didn't say anything as they left the Den after enjoying dinner with Luke, Kade, and their guests. In fact, she didn't say anything until they stood on the porch of their cabin. She turned and pressed up against his chest.

"It's a beautiful night."

He kissed her long and slow until she made that sweet little moan that made his cock throb. "Not as beautiful as you are, babe."

She grinned with the compliment, but she was not to be swayed. Not that he wanted her to be. "Are you still going to keep your promise?"

"Absolutely. Are you ready?"

Harper nodded, so he took her hand and led her back down the steps. Instead of following the path, he turned and led her into the woods. With the full moon, it was a bright night, but in the thick of the trees, it was dark and the shadows danced all around them. She squeezed his hand tighter, but he knew she wasn't scared.

If anything, he was more nervous than she was, but there was no way he was going to let her know that. They walked in silence until they reached the small clearing that he knew was far enough from the main lodge and any prying eyes—not that any of their guests would be wandering around in the middle of the night, particularly so far out. Still. It was better to be safe.

Axel turned to her and pulled his mate tight to him. "Ready?"

She nodded against his chest. "I am."

"Are you nervous?"

They'd spoken a few times about the idea that maybe Harper might be able to shift. He never would have thought it possible considering she wasn't a full-blooded shifter, but the more they were together, the more her own bear rose to the surface. And she was strong. When she asked him about it, he was more than willing to test the theory.

"I'm not," she said. "Should I be?"

He shook his head and his lips curled into a smile. "Not at all. Remember what we talked about?"

She nodded.

"When do you feel your bear the most?" He already knew the answer, but he liked to hear her say it.

"When we're making love."

His cock twitched. He'd never get enough of her. But that would have to wait. Harper's bear approached the surface when they were together, but it wasn't ideal for shifting. So he had a different plan. He reached for her, drawing her back to him again, and kissed her. It was mere seconds before he felt her melt into his arms. She was always so ready for him, so giving of herself.

Without breaking their kiss, he slowly and carefully stripped her of her clothes, pulling away only long enough to pull her sweater over her head. When she was naked, he let his hands travel the length of her, caressing and stroking all her luscious curves.

Then she had her hands on him, tugging at his clothes. He complied by helping her relieve himself of his jeans and t-shirt, but he wouldn't give her what she wanted. Not totally. Her neck where he'd bit her was mostly healed, but the silver scars that would remain as his mark gleamed in the moonlight.

His.

"I need you, Axel." She rubbed closer to him, pressing herself enticingly into him. It took all his self-control not to give her exactly what she wanted. What he wanted himself.

Instead, he moved one hand down her side, cupped her ass briefly before sliding between her legs. His fingers nudged her thighs apart and found their goal. He slipped through her wetness and pressed against her nub before sliding easily inside her.

Just the way he knew she would, Harper threw her head back and was immediately and completely consumed by the sensations he gave her. She was so unbelievably receptive to him and his touch. There was nothing hotter than watching her come so completely undone. Except for maybe one thing...

Axel increased the pace of his fingers, driving them home again and again until Harper screamed out her pleasure. Her nails dug sharply into his back, and he knew her bear was close. "That's it, babe. Let it out. Give in to it."

And then she did. So easily and beautifully, just like everything else about her. Axel took a small step back to give her the space she needed to shift, and there in front of him was easily the most beautiful brown bear he'd ever seen. Her light, almost golden, fur shimmered in the moonlight. He hadn't been sure about what type of bear she was until that moment. She was perfect.

An instant later, Axel shifted into his bear and nuzzled into her thick fur.

"You're beautiful," he communicated.

"You can—I can—"

"We're mates." A simple explanation, but it was all that was needed.

Being that it was her first time, and she was only a half-blooded shifter, Axel didn't know how long she'd be able to keep her bear, so he planned to take full advantage of it.

"Ready?"

She nodded her beautiful golden head, knowing exactly what he was asking. Taking the lead, Harper turned and as if she'd been doing it her whole life, let her bear run.

Axel matched his mate, running side by side with her along the ridge. The cool night air flowed through their fur as their bears ran free and later, when she couldn't sustain it any longer, and they collapsed on the forest floor together, looking up at the stars, Axel held his mate and stroked her hair while she fell asleep on his chest. Right where she belonged. Perfectly content and protected in his arms.

THE END

If you enjoyed His to Protect you'll love Luke's story, His to Seduce, coming SOON. Read on for an exclusive raw sneak peek!

Make sure you visit Elena Aitken on her website at:
www.elenaaitken.com

And hang out with her on her Facebook page for up-to-date information on the release of this new series.

https://www.facebook.com/elenaaitken.author

Acknowledgments

The first and most important thank you is always to you—the reader. Words cannot express how thankful I am that you choose to read my books and share in my stories with me. Every single one of you make it possible for me to live my dream every day. Thank you.

Although writing is a solitary activity, I never feel alone because I have the best group of ladies in my corner that are always only a text message away. Steena Holmes, Dara Lee Snow and Trish Loye, you are all amazing and what we have is so special. Thank you for believing in me, especially when I don't.

And extra thank you to Trish for being my book doctor and being my early set of eyes. Your feedback, as always, was invaluable.

HUGE thank you to Jennifer Wood for being the best assistant and an awesome friend. Your ability to catch all the balls I drop is amazing.

A huge thank you to my number one fans (even though they don't read my books) and the most important people in my life—my amazing kids. Taking on the task of cooking dinners so mom can work, believing in *my bears* and fuelling me with hugs and coffee. Thank you. You are truly the best kids EVER!

And finally, to my very own mountain man, Ike Edwards. For listening to all the (sometimes) boring details of this business, understanding when I have to work on weekends, giving me such valuable assistance with cover images and potential plot points (ha ha), providing inspiration for my alpha male heroes and believing in me.

I have the best job in the world because I get to write the stories of my heart and it's my hope that you enjoy reading them as much as I love writing them. Whenever I get the chance, I escape to the mountains to soak up the inspiration and plot my next story.

To learn more about Elena Aitken and her other books, please visit www.elenaaitken.com
Twitter - @elenaaitken
Facebook - www.facebook.com/elenaaitken.author

Please enjoy this exclusive *raw* unedited excerpt from His to Seduce, the second book in the Bears of Grizzly Ridge Series, coming late winter 2016!

His to Protect

CHAPTER 1

For Chloe Karrington there was nothing better than walking through the forest. The way the sun danced and played in the branches of the pines as she walked, the cushion of the needles beneath her feet, the fresh, crisp air she inhaled deeply into her lungs.

No. There was nothing better than a walk through the forest.

Unless it was a run.

She glanced around. She was alone.

She could shift into her bear. The need to release her animal bristled just below the surface, but she pushed it down. There were certain things she could do, and certain things she couldn't. And letting her bear loose in an unknown forest was most definitely in the *couldn't* category.

But maybe...

She let her mind drift as she checked our her surroundings.

There was no one around. And she already knew there were bears on Grizzly Ridge. Beside the obviousness of the name, it was well known in the bear community that the Jackson brothers had been exiled from their clan and had

v

settled on the ridge instead. Besides, no one would see her if she was careful.

"No." She stamped her foot to make her point. "Pull it together, Chloe. You're working."

She straightened her shoulders, and flipped her dark braid over her shoulder. If there was one thing Chloe prided herself on, it was her professionalism. As an environmental impact researcher, she took her job extremely seriously. Especially since the very thing she always seemed to find herself researching was the very habitat she craved the most. That, and if she did screw up, the ramifications could be very serious. Maybe even life threatening. Chloe flipped open her leather bound notebook and stared at the newspaper clipping she'd taped into the cover as a constant reminder.

Her fingers traced the faded photo of little Jordan Adams.

Only five years old.

Yes, she reminded herself. There were consequences to making mistakes. Mistakes she'd never make again.

She liked to be reminded of the past, but only to the extent that it kept her on her toes. Mostly, Chloe was happy to put the past behind her. *Way* behind her. She tucked the book back into the canvas cross body bag she always wore and continued walking.

It was more than just a recreational hike, but more of a recognizance mission as she made her first journey out onto Grizzly Ridge. Later that afternoon, Chloe would drive up the road, park in front of the buildings and formally introduce herself to the Jackson brothers that ran the adventure tourism lodge on the ridge, but for the moment she was enjoying the peace and allowing herself to form her own opinion of the operation. It was a technique she liked to use whenever she had the opportunity. Besides, there was a chance that as soon as she made it known that she was there to investigate complaints of environmental disruption, she might not be Grizzly Ridge's most popular guest. And the opportunity to investigate the area on her own would definitely be gone.

She walked for a few more minutes, letting her mind clear. It didn't take long for Chloe's bear to sneak up toward the surface of her consciousness again. How long had it been since she'd run?

Weeks? Months?

Too long. *Way* too long.

Ironically, she'd originally taken the job because of the ability to be outdoors. It had seemed like a good way to satisfy the animal inside her. What she hadn't anticipated was that despite the time outdoors, there was less time to let her bear out than she'd thought. But, as it turned out, there were other benefits to the job. Like being alone. Her family would like nothing more than to see her settle down and have her own cubs. Chloe was lucky her parents weren't traditional in their thinking. They were more than happy for her to pick her own mate.

As long as she picked one.

She shook her head.

The last thing she needed was someone tying her down, telling her what to do and keeping her barefoot and pregnant.

No thanks.

Ever since she was little, Chloe had been fiercely independent. She could handle herself, and that's exactly what she did. She saw the way her older cousins and sisters changed themselves for the males in their life. Becoming giggly and stupid, pretending they couldn't open jars of pickles. *What was that all about?* She could open her own jar of pickles thank you very much.

No male needed.

Not that her parents understood that. Which is why her career was perfect. She moved around so much from one job to the next that she'd effectively made herself a very undesirable partner. After all, not many strong, alpha males liked a woman with a serious career. At least none she'd found.

It was the perfect explanation for her mom and dad and for the most part they seemed to understand, even if they couldn't totally wrap their heads around the idea that Chloe was choosing to be alone.

The thing was, as much as she didn't want to admit it, even to herself…Chloe didn't want to be alone. Not really.

She was so wrapped up in her thoughts as she walked, Chloe hardly noticed that the thick pines were thinning. Not until she stepped out onto the ridge. The blue of the sky stretched out before her, the view of the mountain range took her breath away.

"Wow." Was all she could manage to say. It was woefully understated, but there was no word to describe the incredible beauty mother nature had laid out before her.

Stunned into silencing her mind, Chloe stood frozen on the ridge and took it all in.

After a few moments of admiring the view, she made a split second decision. It wasn't the most responsible thing to do, but…screw responsible. She needed to experience this amazing place in all the glory it really had to offer. And there was only one way she knew to do that.

She was careful to fold her clothes and her tuck her bag next to a tree. Then, naked, Chloe took a step and stretched her arms up overhead. The moments before she shifted into her bear had always been the only time Chloe was comfortable in her curvy human body. Her thick thighs, and ample chest were nothing but a hindrance in her daily life, but in those moments, they felt almost sensuous. And then, a second later, Chloe exhaled and started running. As she moved, her body morphed seamlessly into a strong, beautiful black bear.

Chloe pushed every thought from her mind and let her lean muscles stretch with the exertion of the run. The cool wind on the ridge whipped through her fur and the feeling of freedom that flowed through every fibre in her body made her feel alive in a way that nothing else had in months.

Soon, she veered from the ridge and into the cover of the trees where she scratched her back against the trunk of a tall pine before rolling in the fragrant forest floor. She was so caught up in herself, she didn't hear the animal approaching until it was too late.

Luke Jackson stared directly into the bluest eyes he'd ever seen on a black bear. Not that he saw many black bears on his ridge. Or, any at all.

The bear hadn't heard him coming but the moment she had, she'd flipped over from where she was rolling in the pine needles like a cub and stared him down, baring her teeth to him with a snarl. The fact that there was a strange female black bear who was maybe half the size of his own massive grizzly, and that female was standing her ground against him, intrigued Luke. A lot.

But not as much as the scent of her. Fresh and crisp like the pine trees they were surrounded by. But something else, too. A white musk that filled the air, and his senses.

Which is why it took him a moment to react the way he should have immediately. Finally, his senses caught up with him. With a roar, Luke reared up on his hind legs in a move that was more threatening than predatory, but he knew it would serve his purpose and scare the intruder away, which is exactly what it did. By the time he'd dropped to all fours, the black bear was gone and to his shock, Luke was disappointed.

Very disappointed.

Luke's role at Grizzly Ridge, the eco-adventure lodge he and his two brothers had opened a few months before, was to lead the hikes and outdoor activities. A perfect fit for him since he'd always felt more at home in the woods that anywhere else. It also meant that he could legitimately sneak away to shift into his bear and run free as frequently as he needed too. Especially now that it was autumn, also known as *bump season*. There weren't many guests for the next few weeks, and the few they had at the moment seemed to be more interested in staying close to the main lodge, also known as the Den.

With his free time, he was supposed to be working on a new fly fishing tour they were going to start offering to guests, but that afternoon Luke couldn't resist the urge to let his bear run. As soon as he'd shifted and his senses were heightened, he recognized that something was different. There was an unrecognizable scent. Another bear. He knew the woods better than anyone. Every sound, every shadow…every scent.

And the scent of a female was definitely unusual on Grizzly Ridge. A few months earlier his older brother, Axel had taken a mate. Luke had recognized right away that Harper was at least part bear, but she'd been totally unaware of it and had never shifted before until after she and Axel had mated. Once she'd discovered her bear, there was no keeping her away from it. Axel and Harper spent a lot of late nights running through the woods. But the scent Luke was picking up on was definitely different than Harper's slightly sweeter smell.

This female was different. His blood ran hotter with every breath in. She filled his senses.

It hadn't taken long to track her. If she'd been trying to hide, she'd done a bad job of it. Luke approached quietly, stalking her. It was always best to tread lightly until one knew what he was dealing with. But when he saw what he *was* dealing with—a black bear who for all intents and purposes looked like she was *playing*. He wasn't sure how to handle it.

And she wasn't just any black bear. She had the most magnificent, shiny dark fur that he'd ever seen. It almost appeared blue where the sun hit it. But not as blue as her eyes. Never before had Luke seen a bear with blue eyes and when she finally noticed him and her gaze locked on his, those eyes flashed with electricity. But it wasn't fear. It was almost a challenge.

A challenge he'd accepted. Although moments after he reared up and roared, causing her to run, he'd regretted it. It was probably for the best. At least that's what Luke kept telling himself as he turned and lumbered back in the direction he'd come from. Back to the Den.

Nothing good could come from a female bear. Particularly one that clouded his senses so quickly and completely the way that little black bear had.

No. It was definitely better that she'd run off.

I hope you enjoyed that little sneak peek!

Made in the USA
Lexington, KY
15 April 2016